The Forty Fathom Bank

AND OTHER STORIES

The Forty Fathom Bank

AND OTHER STORIES

Les Galloway

Afterword by Jerome Gold

CHRONICLE BOOKS

SAN FRANCISCO

Some of the stories in this collection have previously appeared in the following magazines: "The Caspar" in *The Arizona Quarterly;* "The Albacore Fisherman" (a shorter version) in *Esquire;* and "Where No Flowers Bloom" in *Prairie Schooner.*

Library of Congress Cataloging-in-Publication Data:
Galloway, Les.
    The forty fathom bank and other stories / Les Galloway ; afterword by Jerome Gold.
p. cm.
ISBN 0-8118-4403-X
    1. Adventure stories, American. 2. Sea stories, American. I. Title.
PS3557.A4156A6 2004
813'.54—dc22   2003019242

Manufactured in the United States of America

Design by Azi Rad
Cover design by Brenda Rae Eno and Tonya Hudson
Typeset by Janis Reed
Typeset in Elmhurst and Stuyvesant

Distributed in Canada by Raincoast Books
9050 Shaughnessy Street
Vancouver, British Columbia V6P 6E5

10 9 8 7 6 5 4 3 2 1

Chronicle Books LLC
85 Second Street
San Francisco, California 94105
www.chroniclebooks.com

Contents

The Forty Fathom Bank

And when he finds that the sum of his transgressions is great he will many a time like a child start up in his sleep, and he is filled with dark forebodings.

~ PLATO, *The Republic*

I

For the first few months I felt nothing, really, except now and then a vague feeling of uneasiness like the after-effect of a dream whose full meaning has escaped in the dark fragments of its own confused scenes. Beyond that, it seldom crossed my mind, and when it did I would tell myself that it was an accident, an accident at sea. I would say it over and over again, like an incantation, and try not to think of anything but the words. That way, I was able to keep it locked up inside me, concealed, so to speak, from my conscious thoughts. And too, I managed to keep myself quite busy, much busier than I needed to be, so that I had little time for reflection.

But one night after all my business was done, when everything was in perfect order, I woke up out of a sound sleep. I just opened my eyes and was wide awake in the middle of the night. After that, nothing did any good.

Now all this was a long time ago, so it would seem only natural that the whole experience, as terrible as it was, should eventually have faded from my mind. But nothing has changed. The old feelings of uneasiness have settled in permanently. Though I have tried a thousand devices to keep them at bay, they slip in without any warning, anywhere, anytime at all, but especially when I happen to be around the docks or small boats or whenever the dank low water smell of the Bay or the ocean catch me off guard—feelings that have gathered a kind of cloudy horror about them as the years go by. And every now and then the memory of Ethan May, faceless as in a dream, slips like a shadow across my mind.

We were living in San Francisco at the time. We still live here. In spite of everything, it is a difficult city to leave. Yet sometimes I think I should have taken the family and moved inland, away from the coast and the water and all the associations: the unpredictable reminders that unleash the hordes of silent apprehensions hidden away in the deepest recesses of my consciousness.

But decisions have always come hard, mainly I suppose because I've never been sure of things. Nor of myself. I was twenty-eight then, nervous, thin, tired all the time and suffering from a kind of hopelessness of spirit I firmly believe came from having been reared by a godfearing grandmother. Her countless tales of fire and damnation, along with a very realistic and abiding fear of poverty had, since my earliest childhood, filled me with gloom and confusion. I learned very young to be afraid of both God and his inscrutable wrath, and of the struggle to survive without money. Goaded by threats of punishment, I recited my prayers, but always with the hope they'd be answered not with guidance or forgiveness, but with money, which even as a child I found more effective in exorcising the evils of this world than the whispered appeals for divine approval.

My grandmother died at eighty-two, sustained to the last by fantasies of eternal bliss in the Four Square City of Gold and a life-long confidence in the Second Coming, but leaving me with nothing but a legacy of self-doubt and confusion to face the worst years of the Depression.

I had nothing, and as I look back it seems that I must have accepted this fact as my way of life, though resentfully and with considerable fear. And being afraid, I took few chances. I clung to things, to the status quo, to my wife, my jobs, and I avoided changes.

Yet sometime before the war, I did something quite

unusual for me. I acquired an old fishing boat. I say acquired because no one in those days, or certainly no one I knew, could afford to buy anything but essentials. It was a big boat, nearly sixty feet long and quite seaworthy despite its weathered look, with a fifteen-ton hold and deck space for a good many tons more. The capacity of the boat, however, had little bearing on its value, for fish at that time brought such a low price that it hardly paid to go out after them.

The boat, called the *Blue Fin*, was part of an estate, and since no one wanted it, I came by it for something like five hundred dollars, to be paid over an indefinite period of time. My intention was to put a railing around it and take out fishing parties on weekends to augment my twenty-five dollars a week income in a real estate office which was always about to go out of business.

Of course, I had another idea in buying the *Blue Fin*, and that was to move aboard with my family on that inevitable day when I couldn't pay the rent on the tiny apartment we were squeezed into, that little prison with its dark, unventilated rooms, its lines of damp clothes in the kitchen and where my two kids woke up to life playing on the bare floors, or outside on the dirty street beneath the endless gray of our San Francisco summers.

As it turned out, the real estate office did not go out of business, but for some reason I was let go anyway. However, by the time I received my last check I had managed, with energy born of desperate necessity, since I knew nothing about boats then, to get the *Blue Fin* in shape and was already running a few fishing parties to partially compensate for the loss of my job.

And this was my life for more than three years, shivering on the dock at two and three o'clock in the fog-wet mornings waiting for a party of firemen or policemen or office workers who sometimes showed up and sometimes didn't. And on the days, and there were more than enough of them, when the boat lay idle I would clean or paint or work on the engine or go around to the bait shops drumming up business.

It was on those no income days as I used to call them, depressed and tired, I would often watch the husky, leathery-skinned Sicilians returning—laughing that good, high-pitched, prolonged laughter that came up from their guts, shouting and cajoling each other from their little blue and white clipper-bowed crab boats—thóse crafty, warm, loud, strong people who could eke a living from the sea and prosper because they were born to it, because their blood and bones and muscles and stomachs and temperaments were adapted for centuries to it. And comparing myself to them I began to believe that my physical frailness—I was five eleven and not much over one hundred and forty pounds— was bound up with our continued poverty.

This thought obsessed me so much I began to have fantasies of doing something wild and dangerous like running Chinamen in from Mexico at five hundred dollars a head or smuggling jewels or even heroin.

Probably I'd still be at it, or something equally profitless, had it not been for the strange and fortuitous business of the sharks that struck the California coast in the fall of 1940 and that, in little more than a year, found me richer than I'd ever dreamed possible.

I said it began in 1940. Actually, that whole dreamlike affair that changed the lives of so many of us, had been building up for some time, ever since the Nazis had invaded Scandinavia and cut off the exportation of North Sea fish and especially of fish liver oil—a vital source of Vitamin A which, at the time, could not be made synthetically. With the threat of a global war hanging over us, neither the cod fisheries in New England nor the halibut catch off the North Pacific coast could begin to fill the demand.

Now all this, it might seem, would have had little bearing on the fishing industry along the California coast where cod are not plentiful and halibut even less so. And since there were no other known fishes which could supply the needed vitamin, it should follow that a windfall from the sea would be highly unlikely.

But one day in the late fall, a small boat pulled up to the Acme Fish Company dock at Fisherman's Wharf. The fishermen had been set-lining for rock fish, but, unfortunately, had run into a school of small gray nurse sharks locally called soupfins because the Chinese use the fins for soup. Aside from that small market, the fish were worthless and considered a pest. And it was only out of sympathy for the fisherman that the buyer contributed five dollars a ton for the catch. His intention, no doubt, was to recoup his loss by selling the carcasses for chicken feed. Two days later that same buyer called the fisherman and offered him fifteen dollars a ton for all he could bring in.

course, the news of such generosity spread quickly
It was soon discovered that the buyer for Acme had,
nd for no other reason than pure curiosity, sent samples
of shark liver to the government laboratory for analysis.
The results showed the Vitamin A concentrate to be sixteen
times greater than that of a prime cod. Furthermore, a
report from the State Bureau of Fisheries disclosed that
the soupfin's liver averaged something like fifteen percent
of the fish's entire body weight! Overnight the price shot
up to fifty dollars. By the end of November when the sharks
disappeared for the winter, they were bringing seventy-five
dollars per ton.

Naturally, the big question in everyone's mind was
whether or not they were going to stay at seventy-five.
There was much talk around the Wharf. Some speculated it
might go up to one hundred; others were convinced it was a
result of war hysteria and that by spring when the sharks
showed up again, they'd be down to their original nothing.
But even the most pessimistic, I noticed, were laying in
coils of quarter-inch manila line. And there was a sudden
shortage of shark hooks in all the supply houses.

Here was my chance, I thought. With spring over four
months away, I'd have plenty of time to get ready. I talked
to my wife.

"Isn't it dangerous?" she asked.

"No more so than taking out parties," I replied, though
at the time, I had almost no idea of what was involved.

"We sure could use the money," she said, plaintively.

There was no doubt about that, I thought, and began
immediately to make plans for converting the *Blue Fin* to
shark fishing. I checked the other boats, talked to fishermen, made sketches of the *Blue Fin*'s deck and hold. I
even sent away to the National Bureau of Fisheries for all

the available literature on sharks, their breeding and migratory habits.

It turned out to be a bigger job than I had thought. The equipment was expensive. The power gurdy that was needed to pull in the fish would have cost more than three hundred dollars. There were coils of manila line to be bought, several thousand hooks plus anchors and floats and hard twist cotton for leaders or ganions as they're called. Any one of a dozen fish buyers would have financed me, I knew. But what if the price of sharks went down to nothing again, I wondered anxiously. What if the boat were impounded for debt?

Winter came on with its week-long rains interspersed with southwest gales that whipped the ocean to a foaming frenzy. Except for some net mending between storms and the usual fleet of intrepid little crab boats that went chunking out in the two A.M. blackness, the Wharf was deserted. Beneath the enervating cover of cold gray skies, the autumn vision of sudden riches from shark livers and Vitamin A soon faded.

The first boat to catch any sharks the following spring was the *Viking* with two men aboard, Karl Hansen and his brother Jon. They had been fishing on Cordell Bank, which is about fifty miles northwest of the Gate. After just two days they returned with ten tons in their hold. News of the catch created a quick resurgence of excitement. When the *Viking* tied up at the Union Fish Company's dock most everyone around hurried down to see what kind of price the sharks would bring.

"I'll bet they don't get over twenty dollars," I remember Joe La Rocca saying.

"Hell they might not even buy 'em," someone else said.

Secretly I hoped he was right. For, though I desperately

needed the money, I still could not face the risks involved, the uncertainties and complications. I felt safe with things the way they were. But I'm sure no one in that crowd of hungry fishermen shared my feelings. A ruddy glow diffused their heavy Sicilian cheeks: their clear, dark, predatory eyes looked on with hawklike alertness. In that atmosphere of greedy expectancy, where the smell of fish entrails mingled with the tang of creosoted pilings and the heavy garlic breath of the fishermen, only one man, a shadowy observer, appeared detached from the whole tense scene. I do not remember what he looked like, only that a feeling of quiescence seemed to emanate from where he was standing, alone, in a far corner of the shed.

Nothing happened until late in the afternoon when half a dozen of the biggest fish buyers in town showed up. With them was a man in a gray business suit whom no one had ever seen before. The twenty or more fishermen who gathered stayed together talking quietly in Italian. Then Karl Hansen, the *Viking*'s owner, climbed up on a box and asked for bids.

"Holy Christ," Joe shouted, "they're going to auction them off."

Tarantino started the bidding at twenty dollars.

"That's about what I figured," someone said, gloomily, "the whole thing was too damned good to be true."

But just then the man in the gray suit said he'd go one hundred.

"He must be off his rocker," Joe said, "or else there's something going on we don't know about."

After that we just stood there with our mouths open, staring, as the bids jumped from two hundred to five hundred to seven hundred.

"Anybody go eight?" Karl Hansen asked tensely.

The man in the gray suit raised his hand then immediately took out his check book and those of us who were close enough saw him hurriedly write out a check for eight thousand dollars. Printed on the check was the name of one of the biggest pharmaceutical houses in the country.

The next minute every fisherman in the place was running for his boat, that is, everyone but me. I was too sick at heart, too filled with despair to care about anything.

After a time I walked down to the *Blue Fin* and sat, disconsolately, in the wheelhouse. Where would it all end, I wondered, close to tears. Why was it that I alone was always singled out for failure? I looked out at the *Blue Fin*'s big afterdeck, at the stout sideboards and the heavy planked hatch cover and thought of the big empty fish hold below. Suddenly my despair turned to anger.

"If you'd get off your dead ass and do something," I said to myself, "you could pull out of this mess in no time. Borrow the money, outfit the boat and get the hell out there before you blow it again."

It was the same kind of thinking that had jolted me into buying the boat in the first place and then into taking out parties. Now, as if I had been brutally slapped into consciousness, the prospects loomed, not only enormous, but easily attainable. Then, as if this wasn't enough to stimulate me to action, just as I was leaving the Wharf I met Joe La Rocca unloading his pick-up.

"You heard the latest?" he asked, excitedly and, without waiting for a reply, "Some nut up in Eureka is paying eighteen hundred dollars a ton," he shouted, jubilantly, "so they've pegged the price at eighteen hundred all along the coast. Think of it," he cried, pounding me on the back, "That's damned near a dollar a pound for them stinkin' sharks."

Perhaps all this was too much for me. Perhaps I didn't really believe it. One way or the other I did nothing. And the weeks passed. I made plans to borrow the money and convert the *Blue Fin*. I talked to fishermen, learned where they'd caught their sharks, studied their fishing gear. I became an expert without ever catching a fish. Yet in my own mind I felt at ease, as if all my financial troubles were over, as if at any time I liked I could just run out the Gate and make my fortune. All that spring I continued to haul fishing parties.

Meanwhile just about everything that could float had put to sea. Purse seiners from Monterey; halibut boats out of Puget Sound with names like *Helga, Leif Erikson, Gjoa;* crab boats and trawlers from Eureka; and salmon trollers from San Francisco, all were fishing sharks. Even rowboats with outboards could be seen far out on the ocean. Many fortunes were made and there were many reports of drownings.

In midsummer, Joe La Rocca bought a new boat, a fifty-foot diesel fully equipped that must have cost ten thousand dollars.

"Take the gear off my old boat," he said expansively, "and get out there before it's too late."

But still I did nothing.

Then two misfortunes befell me almost at once. An amendment to a law regarding party boat licensing had been passed. Through some oversight on my part, I'd failed to comply with the new regulations and my license was revoked. That very night when I got home, my wife announced she was pregnant again.

It was already late in October. The shark fishing season, I knew, would soon be over. Yet, once again, with the energy born of desperate necessity, I installed the power gurdy from Joe La Rocca's old boat, got together the necessary fishing gear and, although I had wasted the best of the spring and summer months, I finally took off for Half Moon Bay some twenty miles down the coast where the shark fishing at that time of the year was best. I went alone, figuring to pick up someone there who knew the water. I anchored off the little town of Princeton on the first of November. It was on the second day of that month I first saw Ethan May.

3

The fish buyer at Princeton told me about him.

"If you want somebody that will get you fish," he said, "get this guy May. He's a weird one but he's honest," the buyer went on. "He'll probably make you some kind of damn fool deal, but if he does, take him up. You won't lose. Only you'd better get out there quick because once we get a south blow, you can figure that'll be the end of the shark fishing for this year. And next year they'll probably be making Vitamin A out of seawater or garbage and sharks won't be worth nothin'."

That afternoon I had passed at least fifty boats working along the twenty fathom bank off Montara and Pillar Point. I had pulled alongside several and they told me they had been averaging better than a half ton per boat per day, and that a few of the bigger boats had gone over a ton. Eighteen-hundred dollars in a single day, I had thought, and had been dizzy with the excitement of it all the way in to the anchorage.

"Get hold of him for me," I said. So the buyer got on the phone and called somewhere and in a few minutes was talking to Ethan May.

"Yeah, sure," I heard the buyer say, "a big boat. Maybe good for twenty tons." I couldn't hear May's voice. "OK, I'll tell him," the buyer said. He hung up and laughed.

"You got yourself a deal," he said. "I told you the guy's weird. He says he'll go out for two days with you and you can have the first three tons if he can have all over that. I figure you'll be damned lucky to get a ton this late in the year, so I said OK."

Three tons, I thought. Fifty-four hundred dollars. I lit a cigarette and tried to appear calm.

"A share for each fisherman and one for the boat is the usual thing." I said, trying to appear professional. "How come he makes an offer like that?"

"Who knows?" the buyer said, a little irritably. "He lives alone. He's got nobody. Probably he gets a kick out of playing his hunches. You got yourself a deal so I wouldn't worry if I was you." He concluded abruptly. "He'll be in on the seven A.M. bus which stops in front of the hotel."

Still in a daze, I left the buyer's office and in the short November twilight, walked out on the pier to watch the boats unload. A long line of them, mostly crab boats, waited in a big half-circle extending a quarter of a mile down the bay. One by one, they came forward and tied up between the mooring floats at the end of the pier so the swells could not smash them against the pilings. The boom from the loading hoist swung out over the fish holds. The men on the boats put slings around the tails of the sharks and the hoist lifted them up in dripping clusters onto the scales on the dock. They were deep water fish, bottom feeding from their sand gills and, as they swung head downward, their air bladders hung like fat red tongues out of their big crescent mouths and their heavy guts pushed forward, swelling out their white, blood-streaked bellies between their big flapping pectoral fins. Hanging that way with their bellies bloated made their long tails look even longer and thinner while their wide set eyes stared sullenly out of their flat, long-snouted, gray-green heads. A man with a broom pushed the blood and dis-gorged slime into the water while the gulls, darkly white in the evening air, swooped down in screaming clouds upon the reeking refuse.

As I stood there on the pier's end with the dark ammonia-like stench peculiar to sharks—a smell I was soon to know more intimately—permeating the darkening air, I gazed at the clusters of blood dripping flesh that by some freak of circumstances were worth some five hundred dollars a sling load. My revulsion and possibly pity for those disfigured brutes jerked so brutally out of their homes in the sea's depths was overcome by thoughts of the load I would be bringing in myself; of the four or perhaps even better than five thousand dollar check I would get from the fish buyer. I thought of how my wife who at that moment was probably feeding my two undernourished children with leftovers from the previous meal's leftovers would react to such unbelievable good fortune.

And then I thought of Ethan May and the strange proposition he'd offered over the telephone. Suddenly the possibility of three tons of sharks seemed very doubtful, in fact impossible, particularly in view of what the boats were presently bringing in. Looking at it practically, I thought a ton, or at most two, would be almost too good to be true. And if we were lucky enough to catch that much, or even after two days the full three, this Ethan May, whoever he was, would get nothing for his work. The fish buyer had said he was honest. But he had also said he was weird. Weird and honest. A strange combination. Yet, whatever, I'd have to take my chances. And at that moment, I had to admit, they looked good.

The following morning I was awake at two A.M. The *Blue Fin* was rolling slowly on the long swells that moved in from the ocean. The anchor chain rasped and grumbled in its iron chock. There was no sound of surf, and I judged it must have been a minus tide because of the strong odor of kelp and exposed rocks along the reef. A November chill was in the still ocean air. There was no point in turning out at that hour, so I lay in the bunk watching the cones of pale moonlight through the starboard ports making erratic circles along the opposite bulkhead. A picture had formed in my mind of what Ethan May looked like, a hulking, brutish man with heavy dark hair and a low forehead, probably of southern European origin, who had changed his name. No matter, I thought—and again a feeling of giddiness came over me—I would take the money, however much it was, and buy some property in the City, a house, or better yet a few good units in a decent district. At least with property we'd have a permanent roof over our heads and with the war scare going on, I was sure to get an excellent buy somewhere.

I got up about four thirty, fried a couple of eggs on the Primus stove in the galley and, after three cups of bitter coffee left from the night before, I rowed over to the pier in the skiff. A cold, clear light suffused the cloudless morning sky above the round black hills to the southeast. The water in the bay was black as was the wide sweep of ocean beyond the reef. A flock of silent gulls, high up and lighted by the sun, flapped seaward. As I walked down the heavy splintered planks on the pier and up over the hard wet sandy beach, the fetid smell of sharks, of sea wrack, of rotted pilings and the high water residue of crude oil was overpowering.

There were some free postcards in the hotel's lobby with a photograph of the hotel, retouched to make it look large and elegant. I addressed one of the cards to my wife and two to the children, wrote a short note to each and left the cards with three cents at the desk to be posted.

I was standing on the hotel porch when Ethan May stepped off the bus at seven o'clock.

The first thing I noticed was the pair of shiny new rubber sea boots he carried tied together and slung over his shoulder. In one hand he held an old black leather suitcase with a piece of cotton clothesline tied around the middle. His other hand was thrust into the pocket of the old flannel slacks he was wearing. He walked over to the foot of the hotel steps and looked up at the porch. The sleeves of his faded blue sport shirt were rolled up tight above his elbows. He had on worn white sneakers, and he did not wear a hat. His head, which was completely bald, seemed unnaturally white in the early morning light. The paleness of his lashes and eyebrows and the unblinking eyes gave his face a simple, childlike look.

"Are you Ethan May?" I asked, surprised and a little disturbed by his appearance.

Without answering, he took a new cellophaned card from his shirt pocket and handed it up to me. It was his commercial fishing license. Ethan May. Address, general delivery, San Francisco, Age, thirty. Five feet seven. Weight, one hundred seventy-five. No hair. Green eyes. American. Single.

He put his suitcase down, took a small black skull cap with a little tassel on it from his trouser pocket, and put it over his bald head. I walked down the steps and handed him back the license. As he picked up the suitcase again, I could see his wide corded wrist and the heavy muscles under the tanned skin on his forearm. And when he looked up I saw that his eyes were pale green, about the color of seawater under a breaking wave.

From the quiet look on his face and the direct, almost innocent look in his pale green eyes, I could get neither an impression of intelligence nor the lack of it. And so far, either from shyness or possibly because there was nothing to be said, he had not opened his mouth.

We crossed the highway and started down the beach toward the pier where the skiff was tied. The sun was up. I could feel it burn into the ring of sunburned skin around the collar of my hickory shirt. Back up under the hills, the shadows were still black. The water in the bay and also the ocean beyond had changed to a deep, inky blue. From across the bay, for the first time that morning, I could hear the low moan of ground swells tumbling over the reef and I could see the green and white water rushing in between the black barnacle covered rocks.

May kept slightly ahead of me, walking with long solid steps, his stout legs driving his sturdy body forward, his white sneakers leaving deep prints in the hard wet sand. The big suitcase swung lightly in one hand and the boots bounced against his calves. With each step, the little tassel on his skull cap bounced about like a small rubber ball. From time to time he looked about with a kind of absent-minded interest, down at the wave-washed sand, at the sky above the rocky headland at Pillar Point, out over the dark blue water. He sniffed the air and squinted toward the sun.

"The weather should be good for a couple of days," he said in a slow, quiet voice, paused, cleared his throat and added, "then it'll probably blow from the south."

Now there was nothing to say to a statement like this. I did not even wonder how he had come to the conclusion there would be a south wind in a couple of days. Ever since I had seen him get off the bus my hopes had been dwindling. The buyer had assured me May was a good fisherman. At the time there was no reason to doubt him. Now I recalled the buyer had been quite abrupt with me. Probably he had sized me up as some young greenhorn and, rather than ignore me entirely, had brushed me off with this fellow Ethan May. As May and I walked down the beach toward the pier, it struck me there was nothing about him except possibly the license he had shown me that had indicated he knew anything at all about fishing. The white sneakers he wore, the worn-out sports clothes, the old suitcase tied with clothesline, the shiny boots, which were obviously new, and now this preposterous prediction about the weather all seemed to point to but one conclusion. He was no fisherman and probably knew nothing at all about boats or the water.

Suddenly I remembered the crazy deal he had made that the first three tons were to be mine, and the thought struck me that I might even be stuck with some kind of a crackpot. A feeling of misgiving came over me, and by the time we had climbed up on the pier and were heading out toward the end where the skiff was tied, I felt that I had just lost my one and only chance to escape the misery my family and I had been forced to endure for so long.

The buyer was standing by the loading hoist when we came up. He was talking to the skipper of a big halibut boat from Seattle that was taking on provisions. Above the mewing of the hungry gulls that arced and crossed in a winged maze above the boat, I heard the skipper saying:

"I think the season is pretty near done." He was a ruddy-faced Swede with fine ash blond hair. "We're going up north to Bodega. If there's nothing there, we try it off Fort Bragg. Then we go home."

Whether or not May had heard what the skipper had said, I couldn't tell. He was looking at a couple of small soupfins that had come off the halibut boat and were lying stiff as dry leather in the bottom of a big fish box. The buyer had glanced up as we approached, but gave no sign that he remembered either May or me.

"I'm going up north myself tonight," the buyer said. "One of the big drug outfits bought out the fish company here. They've been doing it all along the coast. My guess is that next summer they'll get together and knock the price down so low on shark liver it'll hardly pay to go out."

4

It was almost eight o'clock when we climbed aboard the *Blue Fin*. Ethan May took his suitcase below and came up in a few minutes wearing a thick cotton sweatshirt, and he had put on his shiny new sea boots. He did not wear the boots with his belt through the loops, but folded down so that the folds came just above his knees. In a leather sheath at his waist he carried a short bladed knife. I went below and started up the big heavy-duty engine, and when I came back on deck, he had already made the skiff fast to the mooring and was standing by to let go the line.

As I headed the *Blue Fin* along the reef toward the harbor entrance, May got up a box of bait from the hold and, sitting on the edge of the hatch, his wide shoulders slightly hunched, his powerful fingers moving with quick precision, he began to work the sardines onto the big shark hooks and set them in neat rows around the rims of the tubs. The sun was well up and beginning to warm the air. The sky was clear and what little breeze there was seemed to come from no particular direction. A dozen or more gulls, some gray and white, some speckled brown, hovered over the stern or swooped down close to the deck, screaming and flapping their wings. High above those squabbling by the stern, one big gray-backed bird with a brilliant white breast glided silently through the clear morning air.

The easy familiarity with which May had handled the boat's gear and the way he was getting the hooks baited and the lines in order began to cheer me up. By the time we had cleared the black spar buoy at the end of the reef and the

Blue Fin lifted her sharp bow into the long swells moving obliquely in from the ocean, I was whistling a little tune softly above the deep heavy beat of the engine. In fact, I remember exactly what I was whistling—*Josephine.* It had been popular when I had first met my wife; and as I whistled, pictures flashed through my mind, of our wedding at the little church in Sausalito, of the birth of our boy at the county hospital and of our little girl at the University medical clinic. Now there'd be a private room on the maternity floor of St. Francis hospital with big bunches of roses from Podesta and Baldocchi for the new one's arrival.

I swung the wheel over and headed the *Blue Fin* due west in the direction of some boats a mile or so off shore and stepped out of the wheelhouse to see how May was doing.

Except for the one statement about the weather, May had said absolutely nothing. Now he looked at me with his pale green eyes and, in the same quiet, slow voice as before: "This time of year," he said, "the sharks usually feed along the forty fathom bank." Then he cleared his throat again and added, "Probably they will be on green sand bottom."

My hope that had been running from hot to cold and back, now disappeared altogether. The best fishermen in the area had been knocking themselves out for months getting sharks. They had probably explored every foot of water as far out as they could get lines to the bottom. If there were any sharks on the forty fathom bank, they would be working out there and not close in as they obviously were. I looked down at the tubs. There were nine of them with a hundred hooks in each and all set in neat rows ready to be put down. A fish on every hook, I reflected, would bring in enough money to feed a family of four for ten years. Unbelievable! At the moment I would have been happy to make enough to cover expenses.

May still sat on the hatch baiting the hooks in the last tub, his deft fingers slipping the barbed points of the big galvanized hooks under the gills and down along the backbones of the fat, silver-bellied sardines that were just beginning to thaw from the crushed ice in the bait box. The intent concentration of his pale eyes on his work and the way his black skull cap with its little bobbing tassel was perched right in the middle of his head reinforced my earlier impression of a childlike simplicity. And as I watched him working steadily at his baiting, I got the feeling that he was not as much interested in the money he might make from the trip as he was in just being there doing something. Even if he were weird and dogmatic with his predictions about the weather and the fish, he certainly knew what he was about.

I went back to the wheel, not quite sure what to do. If I'd had any experience at all with sharks, or for that matter with any kind of offshore fishing besides salmon trolling with sport fishermen, I could have made my own decision about where we would put down the lines. As it was, I was pretty much dependent upon him. By now we were far enough out so that I could get a good look around. But I could see no more than a half dozen boats. They were scattered over several miles of a roughly north to south line. Beyond, in deep water, I could see nothing. I leaned over and shouted through the wheelhouse door.

"We'll try the first set along here," I said with as much authority as I could get into my voice, "anywhere in between these boats. It's probably pretty close to twenty fathoms now." I had no idea how deep it was and felt immediately that May knew I hadn't either.

May did not answer, but went on methodically baiting the remaining tubs. Then he got up, and after washing his hands in a bucket of seawater he had pulled over the side and sluicing down the deck, he went aft with one of the red buoy kegs, a bamboo pole with a flag for a marker, and stood quietly by the stern roller waiting for me to cut the speed. The squealing of the gulls was like a net of shrill sound overhead. Only the big gray-backed bird with the brilliant white breast stayed aloft, passing now and then across the wake, or without the slightest movement of his wings, glided serenely ahead, high above the bow.

When May had dropped the keg, and the bamboo pole had snapped up straight with its little black pennant waving in the light breeze, the new manila line began to pay out smoothly over the stern roller. May made fast a light anchor at the end of the buoy line, and then the main line from the first of the tubs started slowly to uncoil. I stood with my hand on the throttle, watching anxiously as the big baited hooks slipped, one by one, from off the tub's rim and slid across the deck and over the roller. May had taken his knife from its sheath and was standing by to cut the stout three-foot ganions that attached the hooks to the line in case one should foul. Just then he motioned to me for more speed. With a kind of nervous uncertainty, I turned up the throttle. As the *Blue Fin* jumped forward, the line snapped taut and the hooks began to whip from the tub with an ominous whishing sound and a sharp crack as the sardines hit the water. From the wheelhouse I could see the pale yellow manila line descending in a long flat arc, and hanging below it, the chain of silver flashing sardines, magnified and distorted in the clear, dark water. When the first tub was empty, May, with one quick movement slipped it aside, and the line in the second tub began to uncoil. The engine pounded steadily, the hooks whipped ominously from the tubs. The gulls, screaming in a blurred frenzy, plunged at the sardines on the hooks or made wild sweeps at the bait box.

Suddenly from high above, the big white breasted gull folded his wings and, dropping like a bullet through the cloud of smaller gulls, snapped up a fat sardine that had just swung over the roller. He shook his head and started to take off when I saw he was hooked. As the line went down he flapped his powerful wings and, for an instant, rose into the air, his hooked beak dragging the ganion up with him, and in that instant two small speckled gulls fell screaming upon him, pecking and tearing at his widespread wings until he disappeared in a swirling gray and white bundle beneath the water.

Whether or not May had seen the gull I could not tell. About the middle of the set, he put on another anchor and a third one when the end buoy line went over with its bamboo pole and the flag for a marker. Then he motioned for me to cut the engine.

I was still thinking about the big gull getting hooked and dragged below. However, there was no more reason, I told myself, for getting sentimental over the death of a bird than for the sardine he had attempted to eat. But for the chance turn that got it into the purse seine net, the sardine would now be breeding in the sea or feeding upon some lesser unfortunate who, in its turn should, by like analysis, have my sympathy also.

I switched off the engine and, still standing in the wheelhouse, looked out on the deck. May, who was washing his hands in the bucket of seawater, seemed to have completely forgotten the big set we had just put down. His unlined face, with its clean tanned skin and quiet green eyes, looked relaxed and peaceful. The unconscious rhythm with which he moved seemed in perfect harmony with the sky, the water and the slow rolling deck upon which he stood. And as I watched him, it occurred to me that never in my life had I known anyone who appeared so free of worry and so serenely detached from the harassments of life.

Yet, whether at the time I admired May's complacence or merely envied it, I do not know; but the quiet pleasure he took, not only in his work but in just the simple business of washing his hands, was having a strangely salutary effect on me. The tension in my muscles and stomach that, until then I'd never quite realized was there, slowly ebbed away and a kind of airy lightness began to flow through my body. The curtain of anxiety that as far back as I could remember had obscured and distorted my vision lifted, and a new and surprisingly beautiful world appeared almost magically before me. The late morning sun that normally would have been nothing more than a disturbing reminder of time wasted made a broad silvery track southward, a liquid pathway over which I could easily imagine myself a child again, skipping excitedly toward some divine kingdom in the sky, while all around me the slow, inbound swells flashed and twinkled as from countless bright trinkets in the blue darkness of the water.

With a feeling of unaccustomed delight, I stepped out on deck. The air was warm and soft, and in the silence of the stopped engine I made a surprising discovery. I could feel the *Blue Fin* floating. I say floating because when the heavy hull, vibrating to the pounding pistons, was moving forward at seven or eight knots, there was no feeling of floating, only a persistent and distracting clamor that numbed the senses. Now as we lay buoyantly lifting and falling on the long swells, the lapping of waves at the waterline, the woody thumping of the rudder post and the muted creaking of planks and timbers, all combined to bring my senses into perfect harmony with the easy motion of the sea around me.

At the time, however, I did not question this curious transition in myself, whether May's influence had wrought the change or if something else, perhaps some natural safety valve, was responsible. The unusual experience of feeling myself fully alive and the unbelievable joy it brought left no room for reflection. With new awareness I gazed out over the water. Close by I could see the buoy keg, bright red and strangely out of place on the wide expanse of blue on which it bobbed, and above it the black flag fluttering languidly on its bamboo pole. Far away and looking no bigger than a period, appearing and disappearing against the pale sky, I could make out the first flag that marked the far end of the line. Between those two flags and stretching over two miles of ocean floor, I knew lay some thousand baited hooks. But the thought of sharks down there, of tonnage, of liver, of Vitamin A, of the war in Europe, of work, of money, seemed to vanish altogether in the cool blue stillness of the day. Even my family, though no more than twenty-odd miles from where I stood, seemed remote as if they were living in another life.

Suddenly I had a deep desire to talk to Ethan May, or possibly not to talk at all, but just sit and eat or maybe smoke a cigarette. I was still standing by the open door of the wheelhouse and May had just gone below. He had taken off his skull cap and put it in his trouser pocket. I followed him down, got the Primus stove going and cooked up some canned stew and made a pot of coffee.

We ate in what I seemed to feel was a kind of friendly silence, with the *Blue Fin* rolling just a little, the portable table open between us, he sitting on the starboard bunk, I opposite and the soft sunlight through the open ports making slow patterns on the white painted bulkheads. May's black suitcase was open beside him and when we had finished our coffee, he brought out a big almond chocolate bar, broke it, and handed me, I think, the larger half. I still remember, after twenty years, how it tasted, of the pleasant, homely feeling I had while eating it, and of the cigarette I smoked and of May's pipe, that short stemmed, heavy bowled, comfortable pipe he filled and tamped with his thick strong fingers and the way he leaned back on the narrow bunk and puffed contentedly until we went up on deck again to bring in the shark line I'd almost forgotten and that had probably soaked too long or had lost its bait to the big red ocean crabs.

Yet once the engine was going and the *Blue Fin*'s big wheel began to churn up a mound of white water astern and a wide ribbon of wake streamed out of the dark, sparkling water, the troubles, fears and complex uncertainties were back in an instant. It was as if they had never left me. I headed toward the first buoy line, and when the flag was alongside, I slowed down while May brought in the keg with the boat hook. So far he made no indication, either by gesture or expression, of what we might expect to catch. He worked with the same quick efficiency as before, a kind of buoyant cheerfulness in his strong, coordinated body. Now, as the buoy line came in over the starboard roller and around the flat, grooved wheel of the power gurdy, my anxiety was such that I could feel my heart beating heavily in my chest. When the anchor was up, I swung the wheel over and put the bow a few points off the direction of the set and then, with one hand on the wheel and my head through the open window, I gazed down at the mainline that was coming in slowly from off the ocean bottom. But as far as I could see down into the wavering depths, the hooks hung clean and empty on their long gan-ions. As the last of the set came in, I caught myself, despite my disappointment, watching tensely for the body of the big gull. But by the empty hooks it was evident the crabs had gotten him. When all was aboard, one small male soupfin lay on the deck along with a few red cod, a couple of worthless leopard sharks and some odds and ends of sticklebacks, smoothhounds and a skate or two. May threw everything back except the cod which we could sell, and, of course, the one soupfin which, when I weighed it on a small spring scale, though it was less than thirty pounds was worth more than twenty-five dollars. A whole week's wages at the real estate office! I looked around for the boats I had seen that morning. All were gone. A thin trail of smoke lay low and quite still on the horizon far off to the west. Beyond that, the ocean was empty. And, except for the soundless passage of the long shimmering swells, there was no movement anywhere. Even the gulls that had been with us all morning had disappeared. And standing there on the *Blue Fin*'s slow rolling deck in the middle of that immense blue emptiness with the sun slanting, as it seemed, by the minute toward the sea, I was aware of such an overwhelming sense of hopelessness that had it not been for Ethan May, who with his same imperturbability was coiling up the last of the buoy lines, I would have turned north and headed back to the Gate.

5

As soon as the gear was in order May began once more the long job of baiting the hooks. Somehow I think he must have suspected how I felt, for I sensed a subtle change in his movements and, though I may have been wrong, a suggestion of concern on his face that seemed, in some particular way, to indicate tacit sympathy. Of course all this was a long time ago, and my thoughts since then may well have colored the accuracy of my memory. I stepped back into the wheelhouse and turned up the throttle.

"Where to now," I shouted back as cheerfully as I could. May put down his work and came in beside me.

"I think we'll have better luck on the forty fathom bank, off Año Nuevo Island," he said in his soft, slow voice. There was not the slightest trace of resentment in his manner, nothing at all to reflect my failure of the morning. "We can try one set today and then set out again early in the morning." He paused to draw a little circle on the chart and then went back to his baiting.

The white conical tower of the light station at Pigeon Point was visible above the water a point or two to the east of south. A few miles beyond, I could see on the chart, was Año Nuevo. Using my homemade parallel rule I drew a line from our present position to the circle May had drawn and set the *Blue Fin* on her course. The distance I figured to be about eighteen miles, which would take some two and a half hours. I studied the area around the circle May had drawn. The chart showed the dark, sinuous line at the edge of the forty fathom bank. The legend indicated a green sand bottom, and close by, mud, green mud, brown mud, and occasionally shell. Westward, the ocean floor dropped abruptly and farther out configurations of pale blue lines showed depths to nineteen hundred fathoms. Here and there names appeared like Pioneer Sea Valley or Guide Seamount; names that told of some sinister terrain far below the depths of light penetration, peaks and valleys in silent blackness and vast deserts of slimy ooze. I lit a cigarette and waited for the hours to pass. Whatever dreams I had had that morning of making a windfall in the shark business had vanished completely by now. My only hope was that we might catch one or two more to pay expenses. But even that looked improbable.

When May finished baiting, he lined up the tubs, got the keg and bamboo pole ready on the after deck, then washed his hands, folded his skull cap and put it into his trouser pocket and went below. He returned in a few minutes, however, with two big navel oranges, handed one to me and sat down on the deck of the wheelhouse. After peeling his orange and flicking the skins expertly through the doorway and over the side, he parted the segments and ate them slowly, one by one. Then, with his back resting comfortably against the bulkhead, he lit his pipe and began to puff away quietly as if he had no care in the world. After a while he put the pipe away, let his bald head droop forward, and the next moment, despite the pounding of the engine directly below him, was fast asleep.

Suddenly I felt very much alone and was tempted to wake May up on some pretext or other. But there was nothing I could think of to ask him. Then it occurred to me that even if he were awake he probably wouldn't say anything anyway. I leaned on the sill of the open window. There was no wind and the sky was so blue it seemed to pulsate. The water had darkened considerably and toward the west looked almost black. The machine-tooled straightness of the horizon was so devoid of even the tiniest irregularity that I found my gaze drifting slowly from one end of the ocean to the other. Actually, there was no need for talking, I thought, at least not out there. My wife and I talked almost all the time. Sometimes we talked all night long. But as I stood there looking for something to see on that empty ocean, I could not remember a single thing we had ever talked about, except possibly our mutual worries over money and even these we hardly ever expressed in so many words. I ate the orange May had given me. Remembering it now, that orange was probably the most succulent and sweetest I'd ever eaten. I lit a cigarette, but since it didn't taste good after the orange I flicked it over the side and watched it swing aft and disappear into the white furrow of the wake.

And then, still looking out over the water, I began to think about the little story of the fisherman and his wife that I had read so often to the children from *Grimm's Fairy Tales.* I pictured the poor fisherman quite clearly, hauling up the big flounder that was an enchanted prince and the flounder saying, "I pray you let me live; what good will it do you to kill me?" When the fisherman returned for succeeding wishes, I remember how the sea had changed from purple and dark blue to gray and was thick, and finally, when he came for his last wish, how the sea came in with black waves as high as church towers and mountains and all with crests of white foam at the top. And thinking about the fairy tale I had read so often made me think of the children and I felt a painful twinge of guilt. And all the while these odd bits of thoughts went through my mind, and the engine pounded, and the *Blue Fin*, rolling slowly, moved steadily out toward the forty fathom bank, Ethan May slept.

When Pigeon Point was off our port quarter and I could just make out what looked like it might be Año Nuevo Island with its tiny white sliver of a light tower, May got up from the deck of the wheelhouse, put on his black skull cap and looked out through the window. Then he came over by the wheel and, after glancing at the chart, suggested we take a sounding. I threw the engine out of gear, got out the lead line and put some tallow in the cup at the bottom of the lead. As the *Blue Fin* drifted in a slow circle, I put the line down. We were in thirty-eight fathoms, and when I brought the lead aboard, there was green mud on the tallow. May took the wheel and headed west, stopping from time to time, while I took the soundings. When the depth showed forty fathoms and green sand was on the tallow, May went aft and let out the buoy line.

6

I used to believe that time would efface certain memories, or at least take the pain out of them. I see now that this was wishful thinking. Time passes and things change. Outwardly I'm no longer what I was. I eat too much, gain weight. I've gotten soft, lost my hair. My wife, who was once quite shapely, is troubled by a figure problem. Her hair has turned gray. Time passes and things change. But, for the most part, they're happy changes. We do not talk all night as we once did. We come and go pretty much as we please. Healthy love exists between us all, a tranquil kind of love engendered by the freedom from anxiety that springs from the security of affluence.

But these doubts, these ugly shadows. They skulk about. I wait but they do not go away. And then one moment off guard, one little rift, and a whole scene appears before me. It is mid-afternoon, cool, bright with a moving shadow under the lee of the *Blue Fin*'s rust-mottled hull. I feel a slow rolling, driving forward, hear the prolonged S sound of the bow wake, the ominous hiss of the up-flung shark hooks. Ethan May's sturdy figure stands framed against the sky. After twenty years, this scene, and one other, cling obstinately, at times obsessively, defying altogether the effacing power of time, and every effort of will.

We were a good five miles offshore. The white sand beaches had sunk below the rim of ocean. Faintly, I could see the broken segments of yellow cliffs extending to the north and south and out of sight. Long hills, round and brown and parted here and there by wide hazy valleys, faded back into the dim gray peaks of the coastal ranges. The smell of land seemed far away. Over the stern roller, the heavy mainline, with its sardine pendants like silver ornaments, descending at a steep angle and disappearing far below the watery darkness, made me acutely conscious of the eerie depths below. At that moment I had but one desire, and that was not for sharks—I'd given up all hope by then—but to be back in the City, back with my wife and the children, however impoverished we might have been, however dismal the future might have looked.

When the set was down and the last buoy line was out, we went below for a bite to eat and some hot coffee. As always, May sluiced down the deck, washed his hands, and after folding his black skull cap and putting it into his trouser pocket, followed me into the galley. Nothing seemed to disturb him. The fact that all the other boats had gone, that we had gotten almost nothing on our first set, that we were now far out on the ocean and completely alone with the end of the season almost on us, all of which had put me into a state close to despair, seemed to affect him not at all.

Nor could I tell how he felt about the gull getting hooked that morning. I could only assume that he took that too, like everything else, as a matter of course. He ate the big salami sandwich I put on the table with obvious relish. And when we had finished our coffee, he settled back for a while with his pipe. Shortly he got up.

"We'd better pick up the line," he said. "It'll be dark soon."

"You think there'll be anything on it?" I asked in a voice that must have shown my nervousness.

"Well, I hope there'll be," he said in his slow soft voice. "We just do the best we can."

I started up the engine and headed the *Blue Fin* back alongside the first marker. May pulled the keg and the pole aboard and the set line followed. I leaned out of the wheelhouse window and squinted down into the water watching as it came up from the bottom. I could see the line bending away into the clear blue darkness and a few bare hooks swinging on the ganions from the taut manila. Then from out of the depths I could see the long, gray-brown body of a soupfin emerge slowly into the underwater sunlight. Further down was another. I jumped back to the wheel, cut the engine to an idle and headed the boat along the line. Then I grabbed a gaff and pulled the shark up onto the deck.

I don't remember how long it took to get the set in, but I remember that it got dark and that either May or I turned on the deck light. Beyond that there was a weird, dream-like quality about everything, the white light overhead, the quick liquid reflections on the black water, the irregular sput and gurgle of the underwater exhaust, some dim stars rotating in drunken circles and the feel of the steel gaff driving into hard live flesh. And there were strange sounds like grunts and sighs, at once human and unearthly, of fleshy turning and twisting, of the fleshy thud of the axe head, the squeak of rubber boots on blood, the impotent slapping and bumping of heavy bodies from the black hold. Yet through the delirium of twisting, sighs and thumpings, the unreality of steel in live flesh, black blood glistening, the thick ammonia stench rising and all enacted in that disk of hard light entombed in night sea darkness, a part of my mind, with machine-like accuracy, was counting . . . one two . . . two . . . two . . . three . . . four . . . five . . . five . . . five . . . six . . . until finally four hundred and eighteen . . . four hundred and eighteen. It was not until I had stumbled into the wheelhouse and scratched the number on a corner of the chart that I came up out of the depths of what seemed an evil, exalting trance and, clinging to the wheel, breathing heavily, I felt for the first time the burning in my back and in my arms and down through my thighs.

When I heard the hollow thump of the buoy keg on the deck, I turned up the throttle and, still in a daze, headed the *Blue Fin* east toward land. For quite some while I could hear May moving about and then the splashing of water as he sluiced down the deck. Presently he was standing beside me, folding his black skull cap preparatory to putting it into his trouser pocket. On his clean tanned face I could detect a slight flush that might have been excitement. But there was no fatigue, no sign of weariness. He could well have just finished a brisk morning walk the way he quietly filled his pipe.

"We can lay in behind Año Nuevo," he said. "It's a rocky bottom but your big kedge anchor will hold all right."

He lit his pipe and the sweet, sharp smell of tobacco filled the wheelhouse. "You go below and rest a bit," he said, and taking the wheel swung it over so that the three quick flashes that were the Año Nuevo Island light came up over the *Blue Fin*'s bow. "Thanks," I mumbled, embarrassed by my evident exhaustion, but happy to stretch out for a few minutes. "Thanks a lot."

Below, the heavy stench of the sharks had already begun to penetrate the galley and the forward cabin. I lay down on one of the bunks and closing my burning eyes began immediately to calculate mentally the weight of the sharks. From what I had heard the males averaged forty-five pounds, the females sixty. Figuring at fifty pounds per shark, it would take a hundred and twenty or more sharks to make three tons. A warm glow spread through my aching limbs. There were more than three times that many sharks in the hold. Five thousand dollars! Five thousand four hundred dollars! And a hundred dollars added for expenses. Fifty-five hundred dollars. At twenty-five dollars a week, that would be two years, three years . . . no, more than four years . . .

I fell into a quick troubled sleep in which fragmental events of the day appeared in garbled, shadowy disorder. Clouds of small speckled gulls descended on the *Blue Fin* and were tearing great hunks of flesh out of some enormous sharks that squirmed on the deck and snapped their huge jaws. A giant gull with gleaming silver armor plate on its breast and giant black-tipped wings had lifted one of the sharks so that it was suspended full length in the air. A long, thin snake was coiled in one of the tubs. Its flat triangular head rested on the tub's rim. A red barbed hook darted in and out of its mouth. And in the middle of all this, his face smeared with chocolate, May lay stretched out on the hatch cover, sound asleep in the dark sunlight.

7

When I woke up the *Blue Fin* was rolling slowly. The engine was stopped and I could hear the anchor chain grinding in its iron chock. May was in the galley cooking something on the Primus stove. He had opened all the ports but, despite the cool breeze and the bulkheads that separated the sharks in the hold from the cabin, the smell was almost too much. I got up feeling dizzy and a little sick to my stomach. May was making up a Joe's Special he had put together from odds and ends—eggs, canned spinach, onions, some leftover rice—he had found in the ice box. A pot of coffee was just coming to a boil. The smell of the food cooking and the good smell of the coffee made me feel better. I got out the folding table, then went up on deck to look around.

The *Blue Fin* was anchored a few hundred yards to the lee of what looked in the bright starlight like a long low island with some dimly lighted buildings toward one end. The light tower was invisible, but at intervals of about a minute a brilliant white beam near the center of the island illuminated the darkness, eclipsed, flashed twice more, then eclipsed again. To the north of the island I could make out the vague white line where swells broke over a long reef. The low rumble of water, though close by, seemed far away. Either I had gotten used to the shark stench or the little night breeze had dissipated it. Suddenly I thought of all the sharks in the hold and again a pleasant, warm tingling spread through my chest. Ever since we had started pulling the set a strange dreamlike quality had pervaded everything. Now as I stood there on the *Blue Fin*'s deck with the night sea sounds around, the chuckle of a lone gull, the low booming surf, the sharp sweeping cry of a killdeer, the quiet lap of water, and above, the unbelievable brilliance of the November sky, the happy reality of it all began to come through to me. From the bottom of my mind, the magic number fifty-five hundred kept repeating itself, rhythmically, like a drum beat or a pulsing heart.

When I went below, May had his Joe's Special on the table. Suddenly I was hungry, starved. The food was excellent and I ate until my stomach hurt, mumbling comments on both. I sensed May's pleasure at my rude compliments though, as always, I could never be quite sure about anything he felt. While I was drinking my coffee and smoking a cigarette, May got two cups from the galley and an old bent corkscrew. Then he opened his suitcase and brought out a bottle of red wine. The kerosene lamp, swinging a little in its gimbals, threw a soft shadowy light over the cabin. From time to time the thump of a shark could be heard, probably stiff now, rolling against the hull.

"Today is my birthday," May said in his same slow voice, and, after straightening the corkscrew with his strong fingers, methodically pulled out the cork.

"Thirty-one?" I asked, remembering his fishing license.

"Thirty-one," he replied. He filled both cups and pushed one across the table to me.

"Well, congratulations," I said. "I feel like it has been my birthday, too."

We raised our cups in the yellow lamplight and drank. The wine was a rich Burgundy and in scarcely more than a minute I could feel my muscles relaxing and a pleasant drowsiness came over me. I kicked off my shoes and pulled up a blanket. The dishes were still on the table. Since May had cooked the dinner, I knew I should clean things up. But I could not budge. I closed my eyes for a moment. My whole body seemed to float away, and though I could hear May moving about and the soft clatter of dishes, I still could not budge. It was only when I heard the double click of May's suitcase being snapped shut that I managed to open my eyes for an instant. And then, guilty as I felt for not having forced myself up, I had to chuckle at the sight of May's stocky frame clad in a pair of red flannel pajamas, like some little boy in a fairy tale, as he reached up to put out the lamp.

The dream was vivid. I was standing in the wheelhouse with my hand on the throttle. There was a big load of rocks in the hold and on the deck. The rocks were covered with little specks of something that looked like mica and glittered in the bright sun. The hull was down almost to the sheer strake and the after deck was awash. The water rushing in and out through the rocks made a sharp hissing sound. Close by lay a low sandy island, apparently far out at sea. May was standing on a small dune watching the boat pull away. He had on his sweatshirt; his new sea boots were turned down. He held his black skull cap in his hand and was quietly puffing on his pipe. In the dream, it was imperative that I leave him there because his additional weight would capsize the boat. I shouted to him that I would be back, but for some reason, either because he could not hear me or was not interested, he just stood there quietly puffing on his pipe. I shouted again, but this time I could not even hear my own voice. I turned up the throttle slowly so that the *Blue Fin* would not go down by the stern. As the little island receded, I realized I was crying. But when I wiped away the tears I found great red streaks on the back of my hand.

When I opened my eyes, I could still hear the sharp hiss of water through the rocks and then the softer grinding of gravel on gravel. For a moment I could not disengage the dream from the unfamiliar reality in which I found myself. Then slowly it came to me that the *Blue Fin* must have swung on her anchor chain and lay in closer to the shore across from Año Nuevo. Little waves, probably after waves from the reef, were washing up on what I could tell now was a shingle beach, rolling the small pebbles and making the hissing sound among the larger rocks. The moon had risen; by its pallid light through the open port, I could see the glass chimney of the kerosene lamp swaying in its gimbals, and again, like on the previous night, erratic circles danced on the bulkhead, the rudder post thumped woodenly and from forward came the rhythmic grumbling of the chain in its iron chock. No sound came from May's bunk, but I could make out the outline of his sleeping figure and even thought I could discern his slow, even breathing. And over everything, like a thick blanket of some noxious gas, lay the dark ammonia stench of the sharks in the hold.

For the first time in what seemed like days, or even months, I thought of my wife and the children. Suddenly I felt a great longing to take them, all at once, in my arms and feel their tender live warmth close to me. Then I thought of how I would break the news to my wife about the fifty-five hundred dollars, and how she would just look at me startled and unbelieving, and then when she saw that I was serious, that I had the signed receipt for the sharks and the amount of money to be paid in cash all stated in writing, of how her eyes would fill with tears. Of course the children would not understand, but they would feel the effects of it soon enough in the good food and the new place to live and in the changed attitude of their parents. Yet, we would have to be careful. Even that much money, though more than I could have saved in a lifetime, could be dissipated all too quickly even on necessities. Actually, it would take four or five times that much and properly invested to guarantee any real security. Fifteen tons would do it. Fifteen tons of soupfin sharks. How odd to be lying awake in the middle of the night in a lonely anchorage mentally balancing the tonnage of sharks against one's future security and happiness. But that was how it was, I thought. Fifteen tons of small gray sharks, and they were all out there somewhere, at that very moment, swimming around, feeding on the forty fathom bank. Yet ten tons of them already were safely stowed in the *Blue Fin*'s hold. Two-thirds of all that I would ever need, and more coming in tomorrow.

Suddenly, like a black shadow, the thought passed over me that three tons belonged to me.

Three tons only. All the rest was Ethan May's and whatever else we might bring in the next day. A kind of silent sickness went through me, a sickness born of envy and fear. But I had more money right now, I reasoned, than I'd ever dreamed of having. This is what I told myself. If it had not been for May, I'd have less than nothing. I would not even have been able to pay for the expenses incurred on the trip to Half Moon Bay. I owed everything to him. But I could not rid myself of the knowledge that there was something like eighteen thousand dollars worth of fish aboard and that better than twelve thousand dollars of that was May's share.

The rumble of the surf on the reef had faded to a low murmur like a far off freight train in the night. The *Blue Fin* must have turned with the tide change, for the pale dancing circles disappeared quite suddenly. In the darkness, the stench of sharks lay heavy on the dank sea air. What would May do with all the money he would get, I wondered. Would he still live in a little furnished room down in the Tenderloin somewhere? For some reason, probably because of the General Delivery address on his fishing license, I pictured him living in a furnished room or in one of those old hotels around Third Street with a public bath down the hall and wooden rockers in the lobby where old men sat and watched the street. And he had no one, the fish buyer said. Most likely his parents were dead or far away in another country. And his tranquil self-sufficiency, that made unnecessary even his need to talk, had probably put marriage completely out. Then what would he do with twelve or fifteen thousand dollars? Gamble it all away? He was a gambler, there was no doubt of that. No one in his right mind would have made a deal like the one he had made with me. And he had made similar deals before and lost. Probably he got a kick out of playing his hunches, the buyer had said. But even if he didn't gamble all his money away, what then? Would he give it away? But to whom? And for what? Certainly it would never go for any useful purpose like feeding and housing a family and getting kids an adequate education. What he'd probably do would be to blow the whole works before the next spring.

This last disturbed me so that I sat up in my bunk and lit a cigarette. Everything seemed so unfair, I thought bitterly. Those who needed nothing always seemed, by some prearrangement, to get everything. Ethan May would probably have been just as happy, just as complacent, if we had gotten no sharks at all. Yet, here he was with more money than he knew what to do with while I, who had a whole family depending on me, came out with a bare fraction of what he would make.

I put out my cigarette and lit another. There must be some way to equalize things. Perhaps I could talk to him, tell him about my situation, about my wife and the children up in the City. He might even be willing to consider making a different arrangement for the next day's fishing. But I quickly discarded the idea. Perhaps, and I wondered about this, perhaps he already knew about me. Or maybe he just didn't care about money and figured I didn't either. One way or another, if he had thought about giving me a larger share, he would already have said so. No, it wouldn't do any good to talk to him, I concluded, and besides, there was something about May that did not invite confidences. Suddenly a picture flashed across my mind of the after deck with its tubs of shark gear, of the big hooks snapping ominously over the stern and the white breasted gull flapping helplessly on the line. An instant surge of fear went through me and I inhaled deeply. The cigarette flared in the dark.

A new thought occurred to me. Everyone had concluded that the season was over, yet we had caught what was probably one of the biggest catches of the year. No doubt we would get more tomorrow. Then what was to prevent me from going out the next day and the day after? No one knew for sure when the weather would change. It could very well continue fair for weeks. And certainly May would be willing, considering what he had already made, to go out for a one-third share, which was common practice. Even if we got a couple of tons a day, in a week's time I would have ten tons or so which, with the three I already had, would give me around twenty thousand dollars. With that much I could manage very nicely. I would invest every bit of it in real estate. In ten years' time the accrued equities would make me independent for life, and in the meantime we would all live decently, like human beings.

I put out my second cigarette and, pulling the blanket up over me, closed my eyes. But I could not sleep, for somehow with the act of closing my eyes, my thoughts, as though held in check by the visible darkness, suddenly went out of control; the events of the day, the gulls, the long lines, the wide shining water, the chocolate, oranges and wine from May's black suitcase, and the dreamlike shark haul under the swinging cargo light all tumbled crazily in my mind. And I was aware too of the low rumble of the surf on the reef, the little waves lapping on the shingle beach, the clanking, thumping and creaking of the *Blue Fin*, the smell of sharks and, through everything, the soft sound of May's breathing from the opposite bunk.

8

It was possibly five o'clock and still quite dark when the springs on May's bunk squeaked. A moment later I heard him throw back the blankets and get up. He lit the kerosene lamp and went into the galley, and I could hear the splash of water as he washed his face. I was wide awake, as I had been for hours. My eyes burned and my body ached, but my mind was clear now as though all my thoughts took flight with the yellow glow from the kerosene lamp. While May was getting into his clothes, I got up and, despite my sore muscles, put on my shoes and started the Primus up. The least I could do, I thought, was to get breakfast on since May had made the Joe's Special the night before. I scrambled some eggs with some chopped up Spam, made a stack of toast, set out the oleo and a half-empty jar of plum jam, and poured the coffee.

We sat opposite one another and ate in what, by now, had become an habitual silence, yet a silence that in many ways I was learning made a better conductor of feelings than words. And upon that silence that bridged our separate thoughts, I sensed something not quite right, some shadow of suspicion in May's mind. All during breakfast I had the feeling he was watching me with those innocent green eyes of his, that possibly he was puzzled or curious or even disappointed. No doubt all this was nothing more than a product of my imagination, a projection of some guilt or other. But whatever, I could not bring myself to look up at him and ate my eggs and Spam with my gaze consciously averted.

The sound of the surf had all but disappeared and the *Blue Fin* lay still and silent as though she were beached. The weather had changed. There was a thickish quality in the air that was not entirely from the settled stench of the sharks. And through the open port a low star glittered fiercely.

Perhaps I was merely suffering the anxiety of a guilty conscience, but the subtle change I'd detected in May's expression continued to disturb me. I was certain with that almost mystic insight that had enabled him to locate the sharks he had seen at a glance all that had been in my mind during the night. No doubt the full meaning of those oppressive dreams and fruitless speculations were as clear to him as they were obscure and confused to me. What satisfaction I'd gotten from my unexpected good fortune was completely forgotten. The clearheadedness I'd experienced earlier vanished.

With the Primus going the cabin was quite warm. Yet I suddenly felt cold. I did not drink my coffee, but sat with the heavy mug cupped in both palms staring at the oily film on the thick black surface. The silence, the unfamiliar lack of motion and the glittering star dilating grotesquely through the thick glass in the portlight lens all combined to add to my growing disquietude and sense of foreboding. Everything around me seemed suddenly strange and unreal. It was as if I'd awakened from a bad dream only to find myself in the grip of another, even more disturbing. And, as in a bad dream, an aura of impending disaster, dark and of unknown magnitude, seemed to lay like a sinister presence, not only over the *Blue Fin*'s cabin, but over the whole vessel as she lay dead quiet at her anchor in the pre-dawn starlight.

Yet I had no cause to feel guilty, I reflected, trying to console myself. My night thoughts could easily be justified, not only by my genuinely desperate needs, but by May's mysterious and possibly suspect deal. As for the dreams, whatever they might have symbolized, they were, unquestionably, just garbled reruns of the day's bizarre events and certainly beyond my conscious control. And besides, when the fishing was done and the sharks unloaded, it would be May with his quiet compassion—taking the wheel when I was exhausted, cooking the dinner and even washing the dishes so I could rest—it would be May with his deep inner joyousness and that almost other-worldly serenity who would walk off with most of the profits. If anyone felt guilty, I concluded indignantly, but at once considerably relieved, it should be May.

In spite of my relief, however, I still did not look up. By the light, sweet odor of tobacco smoke I knew May had finished his breakfast. I heard him gather up the plates from the table and set them quietly on the sink, then caught a quick glimpse of his gray sweatshirt as he disappeared up the companionway ladder. If he had suspected anything, either by my expression or behavior, I thought, he certainly did not show it. His lithe, strong body and light step seemed, as always, all innocence and goodwill.

The star was gone from the portlight, and, though the sky was still quite black, I could sense the approach of dawn. My coffee was cold. I put the cup down and lit a cigarette. With May already on deck, probably getting the sardines out of the hold, I knew we'd soon be heading back to the forty fathom bank.

But I felt no desire, or rather, could find no good reason to get up. My thoughts seemed to be groping about for something to hold onto. I tried to visualize the coming day with the sets down and the boat rolling slowly on the long swells, or May leaning back in the shadow of the wheelhouse smoking his pipe, or maybe dozing a bit. But all I could see was the chart with its myriad symbols and long curving lines marking out the seaward edges of these silent black terraces that descended ever deeper into the abyssal gloom.

No sound came from above; no doubt May was sitting on the hatch baiting the hooks, getting himself ready for another big catch, possibly half again what was already in the hold. My stomach tightened unpleasantly. I found myself hoping, almost desperately, that the sharks had disappeared and nothing was left on the bottom but green sand and crabs.

Suddenly I wished I'd never seen a shark, that livers and Vitamin A, my tantalizing dream of wealth and especially May, with his shrewdly calculated deal, had never existed. But despite my wish, I could not rid myself of the shadowy forms that kept twisting and turning in the murky depths of my consciousness.

Goddamn May and his lousy deal! And there was no way out of it, nothing to do all day but pull in May's sharks and watch him get richer. The tightness in my stomach spread to my chest. My throat constricted. Tears welled up in my eyes. And all the while May, serene in his self-detachment and childlike simplicity, was up there on the deck probably smoking his pipe in the fading starlight, completely oblivious to my suffering.

Or was he?

Slowly, and deep in my mind, eerie thoughts began to take shape. Who was this Ethan May, I asked myself. He was weird but honest, was all the buyer had said. And he lived alone. But where alone with no address but a P.O. box and no home or family that he ever mentioned? Where had he come from with those just bought sea boots and a brand new fishing license? How had he known where the sharks would be and that a storm was coming? And where would he go when he left with all his money? The questions came rapidly like an interrogation I sensed was moving, inexorably, toward some ominous disclosure I did not want to know about. What if that mysterious deal of May's were not the long shot gamble it appeared to be or May, himself, the honest fisherman the buyer had claimed he was?

A creeping feeling came over me as tales told to me in childhood by that ancient, godfearing grandmother of mine emerged from the misty recesses of my mind, whispered accounts of mysterious strangers, God's secret agents, who wandered eternally over the byways and through the outlands of the earth searching out the evil in men's souls, of how they tempted the wicked with visions of gold and precious jewels to expose the greed in their hearts.

Of course all this was pure nonsense, I tried to tell myself, nothing more than an old woman's fears venting themselves in primitive superstitions. But my breathing had slowed almost to a stop and my whole body felt suddenly hollow. Nervously I spread the fingers of one hand on the table as if to find in it some evidence of my innocence. The hand, unwashed since the morning before, was dark with accumulated grime. A thin crust of dried shark's blood still clung to the sides of the fingernails. For a moment I could not accept it as my own. Then slowly, and for the first time, it occurred to me that my hands had always been dirty, grubby and sticky as a child and never quite clean as an adult. In its sordidness, my outspread hand seemed somehow to reflect the values and aspirations, the sickly hopes and dreams I had always lived by.

Suddenly, and with the ineluctable clarity of a revelation, my whole life rose up before me, a bleak montage of fears and failures, of self-deceit and rationalizations, of fantasies of ill-gotten wealth and of whimpering self-pity. And coiled in the depths of this spiritual morass I could see quite clearly the unfounded suspicions that had begun with my first relationship with May and that had culminated in the lethal envy of those malevolent night dreams of mine.

Yet this shocking recognition, this beholding of myself stripped naked and defenseless, instead of destroying me as it could well have done, or driving me deeper into even more secure defenses, was like a resurrection or a new birth into a world devoid of evil.

The yellow flames in the kerosene lamps had begun to pale. Imperceptibly the black shadows on the painted bulkheads faded into the amorphous shades of dawn. The long night vanished, and in the cool morning light all my confusion and guilt, my deadly dreams and hallucinations seemed to vanish with it. I felt suddenly free, and, I believe for the second time in my life, buoyant. From above I could hear the scratchy sound of a bait box being dragged across the deck and then the familiar, sweeping cry of gulls, no doubt circling and swooping over the stern.

As I stubbed out the cigarette that had burned, unsmoked, almost to my fingertips, I thought of my share of the sharks and the unbelievable fifty-five hundred dollars. The upsurge of pure joy was almost more than I could bear. I went into the galley, scrubbed my hands with scouring powder and brown soap, then gathered up the dishes and washed them quickly. Filled with a marvelous new energy I hurried up on deck concerned now as to how May might have reacted to my strange behavior.

As I'd expected, he was sitting on the hatch, busy with his baiting. His skull cap, cocked jauntily to one side, gave his face a kind of carefree, almost cavalier air that was made even more pronounced by the shadow of a beard.

Only the tassel, which by now had acquired a personality of its own, hung limp on its string like a little dead puppet.

By the tubs which were already baited, I knew I must have been sitting at the table for more than half an hour. Considering the phenomenally high value of the catch aboard, the lonely anchorage and the still lonelier sea on which we'd soon be fishing, most anyone, and especially May with his acute perception, would have found my prolonged and sullen withdrawal at breakfast, at the very least, suspicious and been on guard. But in the quiet smile that greeted me as I stepped out on deck, I could sense no fear whatever. Not even a slight uncertainty. He seemed pleased to see me. And in his thoughtful green eyes, darker now in the early light, I thought I detected a kind of affectionate concern and understanding which later, oddly enough, I chose to interpret as forgiveness.

Yet whether I was again projecting my own special needs into an omnipotent personality I could well have created myself, or whether May, in truth, was all my panicked conscience had revealed him to be, I have never been quite sure. One way or the other, it didn't matter. The last obstacle to my new found joy seemed to have vanished as completely as had my agonizing night thoughts when dawn came. And, for the moment, I thought no more about it. As I went below to start the engine, the tormenting question of how many fish we'd catch or who would make the profit seemed suddenly of no importance. All I could wish for I seemed already to have.

9

I had always taken pride in my ability to get the engine started. But that morning I had trouble. I pulled on the heavy flywheel until my arms were numb. I could not get a single cough out of it. I removed the igniters and cleaned the points with a file, primed the cylinders with raw gas, blew out the fuel line, checked the carburetor, cleaned the sediment bowl and pulled again. But in the pig-headed way old engines have of demonstrating their independence, and always when they're most needed, the fool thing remained as inert as though it were a solid block of iron.

Finally, sweating and exhausted before the day had even begun, I went back on deck. The sun was up and the air kind of muggy. A white haze covered the sky. May still sat on the hatch baiting. He had rolled up the sleeves of his old sweatshirt and the fine blond hairs gleamed like gold filaments on the clean, tanned skin of his forearms. As he bent over the tub with his legs outspread, I noticed his new sea boots were turned down as usual so the folds came just below his knees, exposing the white fabric of the inner lining. When he saw me come up he stopped baiting, washed his hands in the bucket of seawater beside him, dried them on a piece of rag tucked into his belt and went below. A moment later I heard him tinkering with the engine.

Though my traumatic experience in the cabin had affected what appeared to be a permanent change in my whole outlook, the eerie feeling I'd had about May was still with me. As I leaned against the wheelhouse smoking a cigarette, I found myself listening with mixed feelings to the dry sucking of the pistons as May spun the flywheel. I wanted to hear the engine start, yet at the same time I half hoped he would fail just as I had. For at this time, any failure on his part would have been proof enough for me of his fallibility and hence assurance of his humanity. To see him come up frustrated and as beat out and greasy as I was, if nothing else, would dispel, I thought, the superstitious fears that had carried over from my frightening revelation.

Suddenly I remembered the chocolate and the orange and how he'd taken the wheel the night before so I could go below and rest, and the wine he'd opened for his birthday, and the red pajamas that had made him look like a little kid, and all at once I felt embarrassed for even having such thoughts inside me. I flicked my cigarette into the water and went down into the engine room again.

Apparently May had gone through the same routine as I had, checking the fuel line, the carburetor and the igniters and pulling on the flywheel. Now he was leaning against the hull looking at the engine with what seemed to me, and for the first time since I had known him, a perplexed frown. His face was sweating and his arms were streaked with grease. And somehow, seeing him leaning against the hull unable to do anything made me feel better. I crawled in beside him and together we stood staring at that stupid hunk of metal that looked for all the world like some impudent brat defying its elders.

Suddenly, just as though the engine had been playing hide the button with us, we both found the trouble at once. The battery clamp had come loose from the terminal. With a shout, I snapped the clamp back where it belonged and May, almost at the same time, gave a heave on the flywheel. The engine started instantly and chugged away as smooth as you please. We went back on deck, both of us laughing kind of quietly at ourselves. And though nothing further was said, the final barrier between us dissolved away.

Soon after we'd pulled up the anchor, the old *Blue Fin*, her engine idling, was rounding the south end of Año Nuevo Island and heading back once more toward the forty fathom bank.

The ocean, despite its flat, oily surface, looked swollen. The early sun through the haze had a slightly yellowish cast. As we cleared the tip of the island, I noticed the light was still on. During the night, its diamond flash had dominated the darkness. Now, in the daylight, it looked weak and ineffectual with a pale red tint in its owl-like lens as it winked out its cycle on top of the white-painted skeleton tower.

I was standing at the wheel thinking rather dreamily of how it would be to fish with May on a permanent basis, of going south with him in the summer for albacore and broadbill, then working north for sharks if they were still in demand. Yet, though I was thinking about this and at the same time was pleasantly aware of the *Blue Fin*'s heavily laden roll as she entered the ocean swells, the island with its rock rimmed beaches ringed by tidal spume and brown sea grasses and its lonely light tower kept intruding with dark persistence into my consciousness like the memory of a place I'd only dreamed of.

Suddenly all my good thoughts vanished and I found myself irresistibly drawn back to a disturbing experience I'd had when I was a child.

I was eight years old at the time. An aunt of mine was going with some fellow who had worked as a lighthouse keeper on Unimak Island up in Alaska. From the stories he told me, it must have been one of the most desolate places in the world, with nothing but rocks along the coast and some kind of tall grass inland. The weather was either so foggy you couldn't see anything, or it was blowing a full gale. The light station and the bleak promontory on which it stood was known as the Roof of Hell. On his annual visit to San Francisco he would usually bring my aunt little gifts from up there, some of which she gave to me, like a colored grass Indian basket, a pair of moccasins made of wiry haired white seal skin (I could still remember the rawhide smell) and some mounted walrus tusks with fine, black-lined etchings of dogs pulling sleds, old sailing ships and some Eskimos spearing walruses. He would tell me about the big Kodiak bears he had hunted, about fishing for giant crabs and migratory salmon.

But the story that impressed me most was the one about a big Japanese freighter that had been abandoned in a storm in the Bering Sea. The wind had driven her on the rocks not far from the lighthouse on Unimak Island. When the storm was over he climbed aboard and looted it of cameras, guns, binoculars, no end of foodstuffs, and even a couple of crates of Christmas tree ornaments so that, just for the hell of it, he had said, he and the other two men at the station cut themselves a tree and celebrated Christmas in the middle of August.

As might be expected, I was pretty much carried away with all this and thought of nothing but getting up there myself. But when I asked him if he would take me with him sometime, he just looked me over and said that that was no place for a skinny little kid like me, but if I ever got bigger and got some beef on me he might give the matter some thought.

I remembered quite clearly how helpless and frustrated he made me feel when he told me this. As a matter of fact I was so filled with rage that, had I been strong enough, I would have killed the lighthouse keeper with my bare hands. In fact, for a long time after I had fantasies of doing just that.

Probably because of the impending change in the weather, the usual flock of excited gulls, sweeping and crying over the stern, was nowhere in sight. I opened the window and listened. Faintly from the rocks on the seaward side of Año Nuevo came the short, hollow bark of a lone sea lion. It was the only sound of life.

May had gone back to his baiting as soon as we had gotten under way. His wide shoulders and heavy arms seemed to fill up his old sweatshirt so that the rounded outline of his powerful muscles could be seen clearly beneath the worn gray cotton. The little black tassel on his perfectly centered skull cap bounced from side to side as he worked, but seemed to have lost all its former gaiety.

By eight o'clock, or thereabouts, we were back in the vicinity of the forty fathom bank. The water, with its faint yellowish cast near shore, now turned to a kind of ominous green. Except for the long low swells, lifting and falling as if in a feverish sleep, there was no movement, at all. We took our soundings and when the tallow on the lead showed green sand and the depth was right on the forty mark, I brought the *Blue Fin* around to a southerly course and May put out the first buoy keg with its bamboo pole and black flag for a marker.

Soon the long set started, hissing ominously as on the day before. Only now I detected an even more sinister quality in the accelerated uncoiling of the blood dark manila as it slithered upward and out of the tubs. In fact, as I remember quite well, everything around me seemed sinister, the pearly haze, the thick morning air and the tumid seawater. And the oppressive closeness of the sky along with the complete dispersion of the familiar and, in its way, comforting hard-lined horizon gave me a feeling of being entombed. I found myself consciously breathing deeper. Even so, I had trouble filling my lungs. But all this, I thought, was probably nothing more than the after effects of my earlier confusion and would soon pass away.

When the baited hooks began their headlong plunge, May, after removing the hatch cover, went aft with his unsheathed knife and stood by the stern roller ready to cut any of the hooks that might foul.

The *Blue Fin* pounded along with hardly a roll, though now and again the bow, catching a swell just right, flung a low spray that disappeared aft with a muffled splash. No shoreline was visible through the haze, but for the first time that morning I felt a faint breeze through the window that was not from the forward motion of the boat. Fortunately it had come just in time to blow the stench from the open hold away from the wheelhouse. Yet the breeze, though no more than a whisper, started me thinking of May's prediction about the weather. Again, as in the cabin, a creepy feeling came over me and a kind of numbing cold spread through my chest. My stomach too began to give me trouble with little burning pains and rolling cramps down low. I turned and looked back at May, half expecting to see some awesome transfiguration or even, hopefully, to discover that he was not there at all and that the entire experience was nothing more than a frightful dream.

But there was no change whatever. May was still standing by the roller balancing himself easily with one foot on the deck, the other resting lightly on the combing. Except for his gray slacks tucked loosely into his sea boots, and his quaint black skull cap with its bobbing tassel, he could have been the model for some Winslow Homer *Portrait of a Fisherman*. Despite my rampant fear and upset stomach, at the sight of his sturdy figure there, his discerning eyes concentrating on the rapidly descending shark line, I was aware of an immediate sense of calm.

Feeling pleasantly sure of myself, I was about to return to the wheel when I noticed that something was wrong. Since I was heading south, the keg with its marker flag should have remained due north on the compass. Instead, it was moving slowly in an easterly direction which could only mean that it had broken loose from the buoy line. Though I knew we could manage with one float, for some reason the sight of the keg drifting off that way disturbed me. I left the wheelhouse, and shouting back to May, pointed toward the keg that was quite small by now but still bright red against the water. But apparently May was already aware of what had happened. He turned, and shrugging unconcernedly, said in his usual quiet voice that we could get along all right with the remaining keg and went back to tending the line.

In spite of his reassurance, I could not rid myself of the uneasiness I felt at the loss of the buoy keg. For the remaining time until the last buoy went over, I kept thinking of the set stretched out two hundred and forty odd feet down in that vast silence and deep gloom with one of its lines cut and the buoy, indifferent and insensible, drifting away and out of sight over the ocean. Though it was not unusual for me to worry unnecessarily about things of little consequence, my concern for the lost keg was out of all proportion to its importance. It even occurred to me that some secret part of my mind might possibly be busy with things I knew nothing of. However, once the engine was stopped and May and I were sitting at the table drinking coffee and eating the last of the bread and some tough-edged Swiss cheese, my uneasiness left me.

"The sharks might hit pretty well today," May said when he had finished eating. He leaned back on the bunk and puffed on his pipe. "I think they know what goes on up here. They know when the weather will change and when feed will get scarce. Probably they have some kind of extra sense we don't know about."

It was the longest single statement I had heard May make. His voice was unreservedly warm, almost chatty, as if he'd finally accepted me as his friend. Suddenly it occurred to me that, quite probably, he'd been as uncertain of me as I had been of him and, until he knew me better, had confined himself to pertinent observations, to the business at hand. He opened his old black suitcase, rummaged about for a moment, and came up with a tablet of writing paper and a new yellow pencil.

"We have enough bait for one short set after this one," he said. "Then we'd better get back before it blows." He broke the cellophane wrapper on the tablet and, carefully squeezing it into a ball, tossed it into the paper bag he had set out for garbage.

Somehow this change in May seemed to clear away the last vestige of mystery surrounding him, revealing, no more nor less, the simple fisherman his license had claimed him to be. With immense relief, I realized I was no longer afraid.

I was reflecting on all this yet at the same time considering the prospect of still another set following the one still to come in. A thousand hooks and another half a thousand more. For the next five or six hours, I pictured myself working in a state of exhaustion hauling in these squirming tons of soupfin sharks. The hold would be full and they'd be all over the decks and probably down in the cabin too. They'd represent more money than most men ever saw in a lifetime. Yet when I was all through, I'd get nothing, absolutely nothing for all my labor. And there wouldn't be another chance tomorrow or probably ever again. There was no doubt about it now, the weather was changing.

Suddenly, like the cellophane wrapper in the garbage bag, I felt myself squeezed into a tight ball. With a rush of anger all my night thoughts returned. I lit a cigarette and flicked the still burning match on the deck.

"This whole damn deal was no good to begin with." My voice was tight and I could almost feel the pallor on my face. "I must have been nuts to have agreed to it."

Anger surged up into my throat. For the first time in my life I didn't want words, but some kind of violence. Then suddenly I could feel the deep flush burning in my cheeks. I glanced at May. He had not even looked up. He opened his tablet on the table, adjusted the black lined paper under the top sheet and, with an expression of serious concentration in his pale green eyes, began printing something in large capital letters. When he had finished with his writing, which turned out to be only his name and address at some hotel on Bush Street, he carefully tore out the paper and, weighting it with a box of Kirby hooks, looked over at me with an expression of such ingenuousness and goodwill that I wondered if possibly my impulsive outburst of a moment before was just a figment of my imagination.

One way or another, it was a disturbing little scene, and I was glad when the *Blue Fin* was under way again and we were heading toward the black flag that marked the set's end and May was setting the tubs in a row alongside the power gurdy preparatory to bringing in the line.

10

The little breeze was strong enough now to dimple the tops of swells and to make the flag flutter on its bamboo pole. As we approached the keg, my head suddenly began to pound and my grip on the wheel got weak. It lasted only a moment and, I suppose, was caused by my thinking about the sharks that might already be on the line. Despite the fact that none of them would belong to me, once I got to thinking about them, my mind seemed to turn immediately into a regular calculating machine. A thousand hooks, I thought. One every fifth hook. Two hundred sharks times fifty pounds would be ten thousand pounds, divided by two came to five tons, multiplied by eighteen hundred would be nine thousand dollars. I went over all this several times, savoring the taste of the final figure which, because of other probabilities such as a shark on every fourth hook and then every third, increased progressively to something like thirty thousand dollars. Then I began to think about May again. I pictured the *Blue Fin* loaded. We were heading back to Princeton. I was at the wheel and May stood beside me smoking his pipe.

"I've been thinking," I imagined May saying in his quiet voice, "that maybe you'd want to sell the *Blue Fin*."

"I'd be willing to sell her," I said. "I'd even be glad to. But it's this way. I have a wife and two kids up in the City and there's a third one coming. I'm not much of a fisherman, but if I didn't have the boat I'd have no way of making a living."

May kept puffing away on his pipe. His familiar sympathy was almost palpable. Finally he said, "I'll make you a deal. You let me have the boat and I'll give you my share of the sharks."

"But that would be more than five times what she's worth, and about fifty times more than I paid for her," I said. "You wouldn't be getting much of a deal."

But when he insisted, saying he had no need for the money, I agreed to let him have the *Blue Fin*. By the time I'd gotten the check with its five perforated figures from the fish company and was heading back to San Francisco on the night bus, the keg was alongside and May was pulling it aboard with the boat hook. In an instant, my little fantasy vanished.

I threw the engine out of gear and stood by the wheel-house door watching the buoy line come up. The little breeze, steadier now and blowing from due south, felt warm on my face and a little moist. Probably a good wind was blowing high up for here and there big patches of blue came through the milky haze that had covered the ocean all morning. The line, snapping little sprays of water, sped upwards in a businesslike manner, silent and tight as a bow string, as May, with his ever-turned-down boots, widespread for balance, received it from off the power gurdy and coiled it in neat hard circles on the deck. When the small kedge anchor, its flukes and shank dark with slime-green mucky sand and exuding the repugnant smell of some strange decay, came over the side, the first shark could be seen turning slowly in the murky water.

Once more, as on the night before, a dreamlike quality came over everything. The long gray snout of the hooked shark shot up from the water, the spatulate pectorals flapping like grotesque ears, the distended belly showed white in the translucent darkness and then, with no pause whatever in the relentless, beltline motion of the thick manila, the whole length of the slow-thrashing, muscular body was dragged out and, with the aid of May's heavy steel gaff, slid through the two vertical guides of the starboard roller. Then May, in what seemed but a single, uninterrupted movement of his strong body, slit open the throat, disengaged the hook and kicked the squirming soupfin clear of the incoming line. I stepped back quickly into the wheelhouse, shoved the gear lever forward and brought the *Blue Fin* about so that the line came in on the lee side a few points off the starboard bow. I set the throttle at a slow idle and went back on deck to help May.

No sooner was the first shark aboard than another was coming over the side. And then another. Without even noticing the rancid blast from below, I began throwing the big, twisting fish into the hold. I ran, dragging the sharks by their tails. I skidded, fell, leaped up and ran again. I counted, not to myself now, but aloud, shouting out the numbers in a chanted beat. And still they came, like from the magic salt mill, a steady, unending flow. In no time at all the hold was full. Sharks spilled out and covered the deck. Once I grabbed May's gaff and, leaning far out, sunk the steel hook deep into live flesh. The thrashing weight unbalanced me and I was half over when May's hand, like a vise on my arm, pulled me back. I fell against the wheelhouse biting air, then was up again and away. In the open hold heaped up sharks writhed, their tails slapping softly, blood sheathed bellies revolving, abrasive, sand-gray and violet backs arching and twisting, crescent, serrated mouths agape in their strange and silent dying. Across the deck dozens more rolled about. Blood-black, phlegmy slime clung to the gunn'ls and sideboards. In the scuppers the bodies of young sharks, disgorged from pregnant females, squirmed weakly like soft, blind tadpoles. Forward beyond the heavy sideboards, a big one twisted and snapped itself into the water. I snatched up the axe and in a frenzy danced about, battering in the heads of every shark that moved. And all the while my skinny body, incited by some demonic fire, darted this way and that, scraggy bearded, uncut hair flying, two days' accreted filth on pants and shirt, leaping, squatting, smashing, killing and shouting out numbers in a shrill voice, all the while May's apocalyptic figure, unperturbed, deliberate and infallible, stood bigger than life, by the grooved iron wheel of the power gurdy, all certitude, all rhythm, a procession of dependabilities like the diurnal tides or the equinoxes.

The set was in and May was clearing away a space for the tubs when I finally began to look around and take notice of things. No less than a thousand soupfin sharks filled the hold, the forepeak and the entire deck from forward of the wheelhouse to the area May had cleared just aft of the hatch. I stumbled inside and threw the engine out of gear, then leaned against the wheelhouse and, with my arm dangling limply, gazed over the monstrous cargo that shortly would be hoisted, slingload by slingload, onto the pier at Princeton, weighed in and evaluated at some forty-five thousand dollars. Yet at the moment, I would have given up everything, my share of the catch and the remote possibility of any of May's share too just to sleep, to sink down right where I stood and drift off into utter forgetfulness.

"We still have time for one short set if you feel up to it," May said, studying the water and the sky to the southwest. He had just finished sloshing his arms and face with seawater from the bucket. Now he shook the water off his hands and came over to the wheelhouse looking as clean and fresh as if he had just bathed. "It probably won't blow much until around dark." His voice was as quiet as ever.

There was no sign of weariness either in his movements or expression, or, any sign of special satisfaction about the forty thousand or so he had made in less than two days. The fact that there were still some working hours left seemed, at the moment, to be his only concern.

The thought of going through the ordeal of another set, even a short one, seemed more than I could take. Besides, I thought bitterly, I would still not get a cent more than my original amount. And then, and for the first time that day, a quick and terrifying image of the big white-breasted gull with its gray-white body twisting in the water passed like something cold across my brain. I flicked my cigarette over the side.

"Well," I said in a thin voice, "I guess we'd better get them while we can."

I did not look at May, but out over the ocean. Except for a few swiftly moving clouds, the sky had cleared. The water, for some reason, had changed to an inky black.

May immediately began getting the set ready. First he separated five of the tubs and, after cutting the line, made the free end fast to the kedge anchor. Then he got out the last of the sardines and started to bait. There was nothing now for me to do, so I went below and put on a pot of coffee. While I waited for the water to boil, I sat down at the table and lit another cigarette. After a couple of drags I stumped it out, scraped off the burnt end, and lit it again. The smoke felt hot in my throat and besides, it was making me sick. But since I didn't want to put it out again, I just sat there holding it and flicking off the ashes. From up forward came the soft thump of a wave against the hull. The *Blue Fin* lurched a little, then righted herself. I glanced up through the open scuttle. A small cloud bundle, crossing under the sun, turned the sky as dark as a winter twilight.

May's sheet of writing paper lay where he had left it on the table. I pushed aside the box of hooks and studied the big, carefully printed letters that filled the entire space between the guide lines. It looked like the efforts of a child learning to write, simple, diligent and unsuspecting. Yet at the same time I could feel there something ultimate, something just beyond my reach but in some way discernible. And looking at it, at the child's simple efforts, I could see May's strong fingers working away, his pale green eyes concentrated and serious, yet neither shadow nor flame. And then I saw him all at once, a composite of remembrances. And seeing him that way, with the mid-afternoon sun fading and brightening and the *Blue Fin* lifting and falling more and more sharply gave me such a quick and poignant feeling of sadness that I had to wipe my eyes with my blood stiffened sleeve to clear away the start of tears. In a moment, the whole feeling passed. Yet I continued to sit there, puzzled and at the same time embarrassed, still flicking the ashes off my unsmoked cigarette and I could only explain my strange melancholy away by the fact that I was probably getting a little hysterical.

The coffee came to a boil, foamed over the sides of the blackened pot and, before I could reach it, put out the flame. I poured in some cold water to settle the grounds and was fumbling around cleaning up the mess when May came below. His face was as placid as ever. He had washed off his sea boots so that the black rubber glistened. Even the fabric lining of the rolled down tops had been well scrubbed.

He took off his skull cap, folded it neatly and slipped it into his trouser pocket before he sat down. There was nothing left in the locker but a half box of salted crackers and the remains of some peanut butter. I put these out on the table along with a couple of cups of the steaming, iodine-colored coffee, and sat down opposite him. But again, as at breakfast and on deck a little while before, I could not look up at him.

By the time I got back in the wheelhouse and May had taken his position aft by the stern roller, the entire aspect of the water had changed. The sea had become the ocean with its cool smell of distance and its vast, curving emptiness. I swung the *Blue Fin* about as the little wind that had picked up came in off the starboard bow. Through the windows that had already caught some spray, I could see here and there along the crests of the dark hills rolling up from the southwest, white tongues snapping skyward with sibilant whisperings, eerie in that big silence, then falling off, making white foam patches down the lee slopes. Though it was still early afternoon, the sun seemed to have gotten smaller and the sky darker. And just above the horizon to the south and west, a low cloud bank, like a weld on the seam between the sky and the water, was now visible.

The area May had cleared was so cluttered from gear that he was forced, in order to keep from stepping into the tubs, to stand with one foot on the gunn'l and the toe of his other foot in one of the scuppers. Since we had but one buoy keg left, he picked up the anchor that was made fast to the end of the set line and, motioning me ahead, tossed it out over the stern with no buoy line. The heavy iron stuck with a soft clunk, the line snapped taught, and then the big hooks, as though suddenly inflamed into fiendish action, leaped hissing from the rims of the tubs, whipped through the rollers and into the waves.

I took a quick check on the compass, then looked out again to the southwest. The cloud bank was higher now, lead gray and flat on top. In the distance, the water looked lumpy, with a kind of confused turbulence as though something were going on below. Close by low, fast-running waves had begun to build. They came on erratically, veering this way and that, yet maintained a general course somewhat oblique to the direction of the big swells. The sun seemed to have drawn back deeper into the sky and to have shrunk to half its normal size. At that moment a wave struck up forward. The *Blue Fin* shuddered, lunged steeply and then the heavy spray crashed with the sound of a dropped barrel on the cabin deck. I pulled the wheel hard to starboard and then turned quickly to see how May had made out.

Nothing had changed. The blood-black line uncoiled with the same angry haste, the upflung hooks hissed evilly in their short fast trip through the rollers and May, bracing himself by some extraordinary muscular counterbalancing, stood poised, hardly swaying, as the stern swung up over the water then fell sharply back. Poised that way with his sheath knife in his hand and his head thrust a little forward, he looked like the cast figure of some classical hero portraying, by means of this quickly changing backdrop, two alternating views of man, the one, intense and alert, a tight spring, in the midst of rushing water, flying hooks and wild, churning wake; the other, when sharply silhouetted against the clear dark sky, a lofty ascendance that could almost have achieved some sort of omniscience or otherworldly purity except for the little black tassel bobbing and tumbling about as merrily as ever linking the two together and making them one.

Suddenly the sky and all the ocean darkened. It lasted only a moment and then it happened. I saw it first only as an obscure movement like a quick shadow or maybe even a thought or a feeling. Yet when I saw it, it was as though I had known all along exactly how it would be, as though I had had a working drawing somewhere in my mind all the time. The rolled down top of one of May's boots had brushed against a tub and a hook had slipped over the cotton fabric lining of the creased edge. It was just lying there. And then four things happened almost at once. My hand flew to the throttle. Automatically my foot went to the reverse gear lever. My mouth opened to shout. And then I froze. I could not speak. I could not move. I could only stare, paralyzed as the big hooks whipped savagely from off the tub's rim, one second per hook, not more and not more than five seconds to the hooked boot. I thought about nothing. I'm sure I thought about nothing. My mind had stopped. Then, as in a dream, a nightmare, the boot rose from the deck, not high, but just as though May were stepping over the stern and out upon the waves. His arms spread wide, his head turned slightly as if to speak. Only nothing was said, nothing at all. His lightly bearded face was as calm as ever. Only now it was gentle. Suddenly the line tangled. The tub leaped off the deck, crashed between the vertical rollers and exploded, scattering its wooden staves in all directions. Then with a soft, wet snap, the line parted.

With a violent surge of energy, I shoved down the reverse gear lever and opened the throttle wide. My heart pounded. Thin whining noises came out of my throat. The *Blue Fin* trembled and the bow began to swing. I leaped across to the door of the wheelhouse and looked over. Deep in the waves I could see the vague twisting bundle of gray and white that was May's sweatshirt and the bald top of his head and then the frayed end of the line, waggling away and out of sight. The black skull cap, top down and partly filled with water, was already half a boat's length away. I threw the engine out of gear and stumbled out onto the heaped up sharks on deck. The spot where May had gone down was lost in an instant. There was nothing anywhere, nothing at all but the silent inbound passage of the waves. A cool, steady wind was blowing now. There was no smell to it, only the feeling that it had come from a long way off, an unspeakable distance, from nowhere and going nowhere.

Suddenly I began to shake, my legs inside my bloody dungarees, my skinny, aching arms, my head, my shoulders. I shook inside. Then my insides seemed to turn to water. My knees went limp and I slipped down quivering upon the deep layer of sharks. For a moment I felt nothing. Then slowly I could feel the abrasive hides, the hard dead flesh beneath and then the viscous slime that enveloped everything and was oozing through my clothes and over my skin. I got up and staggered back into the wheelhouse, holding my hands far in front of me. A clean damp rag lay folded neatly beside the compass box. It was May's rag. I picked it up and began to clean myself. Soon the rag was thick with slime. I wadded it into a ball and flung it over the side, then went back to the wheel. A strange quiescence came over me; all feeling seemed numb or dead. Yet I could think quite clearly. I studied the sky. A few ragged clouds, forerunners of the great dark bank now high above the horizon, sped eastward. Probably it was one of these that had caused the momentary darkness a while before. The wind was blowing harder now, and the swells, with their mountainous crests and deep, black valleys, were traversed by row upon row of fast moving waves. I pulled the wheel over and, with the *Blue Fin* rolling heavily under her huge load of sharks, headed back toward Half Moon Bay. At that moment, another cloud crossed the sun and blotted out everything. Then, just for an instant, a picture flashed into my mind of the long and empty darkness ahead.

Where No Flowers Bloom

The sky was clear and I could see the mast moving slowly like a tall shadow under the stars. The pale yellow flame of the riding light, swinging a little on the halyards, gleamed darkly on the orange-varnished mast high above the top spreaders. In the last of the dying breeze I could still smell the sweet fragrance of wild hay and clover from the Channel Islands now far astern. The long, deep-breasted swells that had rolled down from the northwest all day had flattened out till they were no more than a gentle lifting and falling like the slow breathing of a deep, dreamless sleep. Ragged trails of blue starlight slashed across the low black slopes and over the horizon a vague luminescence glowed with a soft light like the afterglow of moonset.

Along toward midnight the fog came up out of the west, high, dark-shadowed, advancing steadily across the sky, bearing in its misty wreaths the cold, salt smell of the sea. In a little while the stars were gone and there was only blackness where the ocean's rim was meant to be.

With the coming of the fog a subtle change came over the sea, an ominous coming to life. I went forward and made certain all was secure, then returned to the cockpit. Down in the water I could see the strange oblate forms of jellyfish swimming. Convulsive movements, darklighted by the phosphorescence. Now and then a school of anchovies flashed by and after them the flame-bound form of some big fast-swimming fish streaked like a rocket streaming fire through the full blackness of oblivion.

All night the boat drifted. The fog closed off the sea from the sky and heavy darkness clung to the water. Yet below the quiet surface, the phosphorescent, starlight-gleaming noctiluca spangled all the downward universe, and constant fire trails marked the silent, deadly passage of the fish.

And all the night I waited, keeping watch for the wind. In the dark hours the waves lapped softly under the transom, and deep in the hull the rudder post thumped from side to side with the dull sound of wood on wood. Below and around the ocean lay like a silent, brutal thing that held within its depths terrible strengths and swift destruction; where the sweetness of life depended on a silver belly against a silvered surface—a green back in a green wave to deceive a watchful eye above; where birth was flung in frantic haste through the saline gloom. A world where no flowers bloomed and no birds sang.

In the misted night, it seemed that the sea was the land's slow enemy encroaching with dire intent upon its shores, breaking and grinding and sucking in with a terrible hunger and cunning in its ways, for at times it stretched out sweet and blue and soft and sang its siren song of wind and waves, luring with plaintive melodies the love-born things of land, enticing with strange perfumes and multicolored patterns of cloud and shadow and little smiling waves. Then with dark treachery it closed in upon them with its gray fogs, ringed them around with horizons bleak and endless, brought down its mighty winds upon them. And when all of nature's wise instincts availed them no longer, and they were terror-broken and helpless in a strange new world, the sea sank back into its primal impassivity and let them die.

And so the night passed like a long, long moment. Then dawn through high fog. A swift flowing in of light—

no certain change, just darkness and then light. And the fog held, uniformly gray, lighted by no single source of emanation, a somber radiance, gray-white and constant from verge to verge.

No wind had come and the fog cast its grayness down upon the dark waters of the sea so that it looked like tarnished black glass. And the sensuous swells, sleek-surfaced and silent, stole down like perfidious caresses and were gone. Close astern a big brown pelican glided low over the water, dropping at times below the level of the swells. Heavy-winged, short-tailed, head pulled in close to its body, its big bill pointed straight ahead, flying with the long, easy flapping and gliding of the offshore sea bird. Higher up, a gull moved through the still air with even wing beats, white breast against the sky. It quartered and turned, sailed down in a velvet spiral and I could see the slate-gray back, dark as the dark ocean.

All around there was silence and calm and I slept for awhile, curled up on the seat of the cockpit. Asleep, yet always aware of the gray vaporous glow of the sky, the dark, unquiet deep below and the wide, level solitude that stretched away to a far-off dim horizon.

Then suddenly and softly I was awakened. A faint breath of air across my face and the light brush of a feathered wing. I opened my eyes and there on the cockpit coaming close to my hand sat a small yellow bird. Bright yellow breast, olive-green above, and the black on its head like a round black velvet cap.

The little bird sat quietly, squatting a little on its pale toothpick legs, head hunched down between its drooping wings, its bright black eyes staring at nothing. I watched for a moment, expecting it to fly away, but it did not move. I reached out toward it and still it did not move. Even the touch of my finger on the soft green feathers of its back caused no more than a slight downward pressing of its small body.

Suddenly it hopped up onto the edge of the cabin and flew up into the mizzen shrouds. I could see it grip the steel cable with its spiderleg feet and skip up the near-vertical wire. Then it flew away out over the water. I sat up and watched it swing in a wide arc around the stern, flying with a loose-winged, darting flight. Once it shot up a few feet above the water and caught some insect in the air. For an instant I saw it flicker, its underwings and breast saffron-flamed against the gray sky. Then it came back to the boat, fluttered down onto the floor of the cockpit and rested.

This was no sea bird, no grays and blacks to merge with water and sky, no powerful wings for distant flight. Beguiled by some subtle witchery of the sea, it was bound now and quickly for the ultimate end.

I watched it for awhile, marveling at the bright black cap, the brilliant yellow of the breast, the soft green back. I thought of the autumn leaves of mountain willows flaming along some quick-flowing river, live oaks, dusky green back in the coastal canyons. I looked out over the water again but there was only the somber, settled grayness of the sky, the gray-blackness of the sea and the long and level horizon that drew eyes along its bleak monotony in an endless, futile quest.

Off to the west a little flurry of wind rippled the water. I could see it approaching in a single narrow lane, dimpling the crests of the swells as it came. Soon I could feel the gentle coolness of it play across my face. The bird hopped up onto the coaming, its small sharp bill pointing into the awakening breeze, the fine feathers stirring a little on its breast. And there it sat, no bigger than a wind-blown thistledown, its black eyes staring dully at the incomprehensible sea.

My night thoughts returned. Suddenly I saw it all clearly, the insidious device, the dark purpose. Out of the northwest, like a fragrant breath, had come delight in the wind; wild hay and clover from the Channel Islands, warm land smells and growing things. And the small bird had gone, following the sweetscented pathway, had flown, down out of the dying autumn canyons to the allurement of new places. High into the setting sun he had gone skipping in the red sunset air, delighting in the wind, following the sweet fragrance of those sea-hidden islands. Then with appalling swiftness the ocean night had come down with its cold salt smell. The scented path dissolved away; the land was gone. The sea turned suddenly black, yawned wide and empty, lay in stealthy waiting till the little yellow wings were wearied out with uncertain flying.

I looked up at the stout fir mast, down along the steel shrouds, at the heavy folds of canvas furled on the boom, at the brass-bound oak wheel in the cockpit, at the great sea birds gliding, wide-winged over the gray sea waves. Strength against the pitiless strength of the sea; the endless battle of the strong. And it seemed to me then that all things of delicate beauty were doomed to quick destruction. I was filled with subtle anger, at the pale-domed fog, at the inexorable sea, at the hopelessness of opposing them. Then the thought came that I might take this lost thing ashore, watch it fly away once more to the wooded canyons above. And the thought was pleasant.

Suddenly the bird flew up again, darted quickly away in pursuit of a minute black speck high over the water. It missed, swung back in a zig-zag path, landed on the gaff tip, its feet slipping on the slick varnish. Then it fluttered down onto the sleeve of my jacket, its dainty wings arched and pointed, throat throbbing.

I looked out over the water again searching for the wind. Soon it would come now, softly at first, growing stronger. I would hoist the sails and the boat would heel over, slip smoothly across the low round hills toward land. I wondered if the clacking blocks, the high spreading canvas would frighten the tiny bird. I thought of catching it, putting it down in the cabin, but there was danger, below, of its breaking its wings against the glass port lights, of being burned on the hot stove in the galley. I picked it up gently, put it back on the cockpit coaming.

A few hundred yards off the stern the pelican was settling down with backward-beating wings on the water over a school of small fish, its wings and tail feathers spread fanwise against the air. Then it swam along slowly, its brown body riding high above the surface. It plunged its powerful bill into the water, then tossed it upward and I could see the flash of a fish held crosswise, its short body vibrating silver in the gray light. Close by, the gull hovered, waiting to snatch the fish before the pelican threw it head-down into its pouch. I could hear the gull's high-pitched crying *ky-arr-kee-kee-kee*, see the big wings outstretched, the black-tipped wing and tail feathers spread wide and flat.

I went below and ate breakfast. When I came back on deck the little yellow bird was still sitting on the cockpit coaming. I scattered some crumbs of toast on the seat, but it did not seem to see the crumbs. I held some in front of it in the palm of my hand but it did not move, only squatted lower so that its tail and breast rested on the coaming, the small, black-capped head down between its shoulders.

The pelican had finished fishing and was resting on the water, its body a compact bundle of brown feathers. Its long bill was pointed downward and held close to its breast. It swam in a big half-circle, its beady-bright eyes on the gull that floated close by. Then slowly it unfolded its great wings, kicked its big webbed feet backward with each wing stroke and rose heavily into the air from the summit of a swell. It circled once, spiraling upward, and soared away into the east toward land. A moment later the gull flapped its long, gray-backed wings, ran along close to the water and was off after the pelican.

The plaintive cry of the gull came back for awhile, clear and sharp across the water. Then suddenly there was no sound and I was aware only of the slow, unwearying rhythm of the surge beneath the boat and the quiet little bird beside me on the coaming.

Then vaguely I was conscious of some moving thing above me. A quick shadow crossed the deck, a flash of bright yellow, and down out of the gray sky came another tiny bird, flying with the same loose-winged, tired flight. Silent as a butterfly, wings fluttering, it landed on the furled sails, its little feet clutching the rough folds of the canvas.

Another came, flying on soundless wings, and then another. Soon fully half a hundred clung to the rigging, the halyards, the spreaders, the folds of the canvas sails, their yellow breasts throbbing, wings drooping.

The females stayed close behind their mates. Drab little puffs of yellow and green, thin little bills, black jewelled eyes shining bright in olive-green heads. And the black-capped males, blazing yellow and green, sat defensively forward even in their final weariness.

The light breezes that had flecked the oily crests of the swells picked up. I could feel the faint coldness of the northwest wind, could smell the salt-sea tang in the air. The free ends of the lines on the pin rail swayed a little and the jib club swung over, dragging the jibsheet block across the deck with a dull, wooden rumble. But the birds sat still. I went forward and hoisted the sails and only those squatting among the folds of canvas or on the halyards flitted away and perched in the mizzen shrouds and up in the top spreaders.

The mainsail and jib filled and the boat picked up steerage-way. I swung the wheel over and headed east. A few yards abeam I saw one of the birds in the water, splashing its wings, lifting its head up and down in quick jerky movements. Beads of heavy wet feathers clung to its breast and throat. Then I saw another bird float by, wings spread wide and limp, and little black-topped head hanging down below the surface. There was no movement, and I knew it was dead. The bird that was struggling made a low rasping cry. With the last of its strength it lifted its body out of the water, flew a short distance over the swells but the sodden weight of its wings soon dragged it down again. As the boat drew away I could see it stop struggling, its head sink lower in the water.

The wind grew stronger and colder as the afternoon passed. The sky cleared and off toward the west the sun shone round and cold above the horizon. The cobalt sea was flecked with white, the slow swells steepened into fast-traveling waves.

The birds ruffled their feathers and hopped along the rigging. Now and then one flew up from the deck or cabin top, perched in some high place and looked out across the sea. Faintly mingled with the cold sea smell was the delicate trace of hay and clover, subtle as perfume, from the islands beyond the northwest rim of the darkened waters. Sweet fragrance in the approaching night, soft land-smells in the rising night wind. The birds grew restless; more flew aloft, sitting close together on the spreaders; clung wind-blown along the hempen strands of the topping lift. Suddenly one of the birds flew out of the rigging and started over the water. It flew straight ahead toward land, then circled uncertainly, started off again, out toward the westward islands.

Then one by one the birds dropped out of the rigging and flew away after the leader. In a little while they were all gone and only the little one on the coaming was left. He had been there since morning, never once moving. Far away and dead ahead I could see the bright pinpoint of light flashing intermittently under the twilight sky on the lighthouse above the harbor. I thought again of catching the little bird, of putting him for the while in the locker under the cockpit seat and letting him go when I reached shore. I reached down slowly as I had done earlier in the morning but suddenly he came to life, flipped his wings and hopped up onto the pinrail. He sat there a moment, the wind shaking the feathers on his wings, parting the yellow feathers on his breast. Then he flew out over the water after the others. For a short time I could see him flying high above the waves, a tiny black spot against the deepening sky. Beyond him I could see the others flying in short shallow sweeps like a flight of woodland swallows across a mountain valley. Then slowly and steadily I could see the little one sinking down toward the wavetops and the sky beyond him growing darker.

Up ahead I could see the channel lights winking green and red, the bow-splashed white water that foamed along the hull. Close astern the waves rose steep. Deep within the dark slopes I could see the first faint fire of the ocean night lights flash and gleam and disappear.

Last Passenger North, or The Doppelganger

May the eye go to the sun, the breath to the wind.
    ~ RIG-VEDA X, *16, 3.*

    Look, look,
    And thou shalt see
    The great immensity
    Enclosing thee.

I

The old wood-hulled steam schooner, *Caspar,* lay alongside the San Francisco Warehouse Company's dock near the entrance to the Third Street channel. A dry north wind blowing steadily over the city stirred the dust in quick little eddies around the corners of the soot-blackened brick warehouse and ruffled the feathers of gulls squatting on the splintered planks. A broken piston rod that had delayed the *Caspar*'s departure by more than twelve hours had been replaced. From her rusted stack a twisting black trunk of crude oil smoke rose into the air to flatten into a dense cloud over the channel.

Captain Larson, or Midnight Larson, as he was known to his shipmates, stretched wearily on his canvas deck chair in the sheltered lee of the fo'c'sle head. The visor of his officer's cap, pulled down to shade his eyes from the sun's glare, cast a shadow over the gray stubble on his cheeks. The *Collected Works of Dostoevsky,* its dog-eared pages and margins filled with pencilled notes, lay open in his lap. He had given the deck crew time off while the engine was being repaired. He regretted having to keep his chief engineer and his two assistants below since he knew the inland heat carried by that unusual north wind made the engine room nearly unbearable. He planned to make up for their unpleasant overtime by extra shore leave in Eureka providing, he reflected anxiously, the engine did not break down again.

To add to his troubles, O'Hare, the company agent, had informed him there would be a passenger on the northbound trip.

"A passenger!" the Captain exclaimed. It was the first passenger the *Caspar* had booked in more than fifteen years.

"Where's he going?"

"Eureka, or possibly as far as Astoria," the agent said. "Beyond that, I can't tell you much more than that he signed his name William Mueller. No local address and no next of kin."

"Could he be going up north to find work in the woods?"

"Not likely. He looked pretty well off. Wore an expensive business suit and carried a briefcase."

"Does he have any baggage? A suitcase, trunk?"

"Nothing but the briefcase. Why do you ask?"

"Seems a bit strange," the Captain commented. "A well-dressed man heading north with no baggage, no particular destination. And on the *Caspar*? What's he look like?"

"He's about your height, gray haired, thin. He sounds educated and speaks in a very low voice." The agent paused. "Come to think of it, I can't remember his face except that it seemed kind of pale. He'll be boarding around noon so you'll see for yourself." He paused again. "By the way, he wants a cabin to himself on the lee side of the ship. Says he has an aversion to the wind."

The Captain explained that since he had never expected to see a passenger again, all the cabins had been taken over for use as paint lockers and general stowage rooms. "Whether or not an accommodation can be made ready on the lee side depends on the whim of the wind. At this time of year, that's about as trustworthy as the *Caspar* herself."

The agent laughed and said he didn't see why it should make much difference anyway.

Though the Captain enjoyed meeting new people, especially from far off places and with interesting backgrounds, the prospect of a stranger aboard, whose suspect appearance augured trouble, exacerbated his present frustrations. And he'd had enough of those. He had been on the move since before dawn hurrying about from the engine room to the machine shop, to the welders, to the company office and back, lifting, carrying, and overseeing things too urgent to be relegated to anyone but himself. In addition to all this, he had personally taken on the job of cleaning and preparing the passenger's cabin for occupancy. A younger man would have found the work hard, the problems difficult. At his age, they were nothing less than exhausting. Now he wished only to rest and to lose himself for a time in dreamless sleep.

From the bridge came the muted clang of the ship's clock. Twelve-thirty. He yawned and closed his book. Two, maybe three hours before sailing. He yawned again, deeply, and shut his eyes. Instantly a kaleidoscope of ghastly scenes flashed through his mind—red flames leaping from the forward hold, a man's arm being torn off in the gears of the windlass. Nameless fears projected themselves visually as infantile memories emerged in vivid detail—a snarling beast springing at him from a dark doorway, a dead man sprawled in a gutter. . . . It was as if all the terrifying experiences in his life were disgorged en masse onto his unprotected consciousness. He longed to rest, and above all, to halt the unprecedented torrent that swept out of nowhere, and like the descending course of his life, raced on without cause or purpose. He was too tired to move and too mentally drained to break the savage continuum.

Yet, despite his inner turbulence, he was not unaware that these rampant feelings, unleashed in a moment of high vulnerability, were the accumulated anxieties of a lifetime of hurrying about, of getting things done, of keeping himself busy searching for answers. With a supreme effort, he opened his eyes. The brilliant sunlight, the comforting reality of the windblown smoke now thinned to a light brown haze, and the tarpaulin covered forehatch battened down and ready for sea, quickly dispelled the morbid flux within him.

A feeling of tranquility came over him, and with it, an almost mystic sense of expectation. It was as if he were on the verge of a momentous revelation in which the sinister and heavily guarded secrets he had lacked the courage to confront were about to be unfolded.

His thoughts returned to the passenger. William Mueller, William Miller, Bill Miller, Jones, John Doe, anyone and no one. A fugitive seeking sanctuary? An emissary on a mission? Yet expectation, whether of good or of bad, he reflected, was far better than the prospect of nothing. It meant change which offered escape from boredom and the ever encroaching desert of ennui.

2

The trip from San Francisco to Astoria took two weeks counting the calls the *Caspar* made at Fort Bragg and Noyo along the Mendocino Coast and at Eureka, Port Orford, Coos Bay and Astoria farther north. For forty-five years the Captain had been making that same run with little to break the monotony except the usual bad weather off Cape Mendocino, which of late made the old wood hull creak and groan and show her years. The routine sameness of sea and sky, of loading and discharging, of bills of lading, of endless loads of redwood and fir swinging up from the docks, the cry of gulls mingling with the hiss and rumble of steam winches together and unvaried, like a single experience, the Captain sometimes reflected, had certainly made his life seem shorter.

Yet his way of life, isolated as it was, had had certain advantages. It had given him time and the peace of mind to read, which was one of his greatest pleasures; also to write in his journal, which he usually did late each night in the privacy of his cabin—hence his nickname, Midnight. He had always considered himself a reasonably happy man, satisfied with his chosen work, productive in that he had served in the development of the coastal lumber industry, and creative in that his journal, much of which had been published in various shipping magazines, was a vivid and running account of nearly a half century of West Coast trading.

But the Captain's capacity for keeping himself constantly busy was by no means innate. He had acquired it through years of strict mental discipline and for the specific purpose of protecting him from certain irrational fears that had troubled his youth, fears that if left unchecked would, he had reason to believe, have expanded into self-destructive phobias. Fortunately, his efforts had been doubly rewarding. He had found immense satisfaction in the acquisition of vast stores of knowledge and, as far as he could tell, his fears had been laid to rest, if not expunged entirely.

Yet lately, and despite his characteristic optimism, he had found himself reflecting on the immense passage of time consumed in those years of service. He could recall with amazement and a certain dismay that he had first shipped out, on that very same vessel, in 1890, in another era really, when passengers, of which there were many then, drove down to the dock in carriages, the women in bustles, the children with ribboned hats and high-buttoned shoes. Men sported gold-headed canes and well-trimmed beards. But he knew very well that retrospection, especially the kind that eulogized the unrecoverable past, could become a dangerous habit at his age. Happily, however, he was not inclined to morose reflection and could dispel the touches of loneliness those memories evoked by the simple process of directing his attention to any one of the numerous activities in which he had always managed to occupy himself. Now the prospect of a passenger, even one of dubious intentions, began to arouse in him a feeling of quiet excitement. He glanced at the dock. Except for the gulls shifting restlessly in the wind, there was no movement anywhere.

He opened his book and turned to *Notes From the Underground* where he had underscored a number of passages for further consideration. With the recently washed-down decks drying in uneven patches around him, he confronted certain thoughts of the author with ideas of his own, subjecting both to a kind of lazy analysis in the enervating heat of the noon sun.

Though the Captain had never enjoyed Dostoevsky, he had read his books, for the most part out of deference to his great reputation. Among the Russians, Tolstoy, Chekov and Gorky appealed to him more deeply because they gave him a feeling that life, despite its superincumbent difficulties and the imposition of an often ugly and unjustifiable fate, did have its bright side, its moments of tenderness and humor, as well as beauty; a feeling which, constitutionally, he was in agreement with. At the moment, however, a certain well-known line in *Notes* caught his interest. "To be too conscious is an illness." But to be too anything could be an illness, he reflected, too ambitious, greedy, lazy, even to be too kind or too generous. He could think of numerous character traits, which, if overdone, could be claimed as an illness of some kind or other. Yet the quality of being too conscious seemed somehow different from the others, set apart, as though it bore upon some basic question, something deeply personal. He would have developed his line of thought, and perhaps written on it in his journal, only now a gentle drowsiness began to lull his mind into less ambitious paths.

He closed the book, placed it beside him on the deck, then lay back on his canvas chair. The heat felt good. It penetrated the heavy material of his uniform and went deep into his muscles. At the moment he could think of nothing more pleasant or desirable. He closed his eyes. The best things in life are free, he thought. And the simplest are the best. Both cliches. Or conventions? One way or another, there was something to be said for them. Or at least for conventions. They saved making decisions with their consequent uncertainties. Why, it even exorcised the guilt of . . . lying in the sun. He smiled drowsily at his thoughts. How childish one becomes when falling asleep. He yawned deeply, luxuriously. And all the while, the dry north wind, hot and strangely tension-producing, continued to blow over the city.

The next moment he slept and in his sleep, the concerns of the day, shunted aside by more pressing thoughts, began to assemble in the shadowy action of dreams. A man who, by the tools weighting his pockets, was obviously a workman from below, appeared darkly on deck. Except for his eyes, which were startlingly white, the man was completely black. He stood in front of the Captain with his sooty hands stretched out as though he were holding something.

"What brings you up here?" the Captain asked. For a moment the man hesitated as though awaiting directions before replying.

"It was bound to happen sooner or later," the man said finally, and the Captain knew the workman was telling him the boiler could not be repaired, that it was worn out like a rotten inner tube or an old man's heart and that the *Caspar* would sail no more. But, though he knew all this, also that the man's empty hands were conclusive evidence of the end of an era and the beginning of something that suddenly caused fear to swell in his chest, the Captain demanded to hear the facts.

The man just stood there, shaking his head.

"It's a difficult habit to break," he said, finally.

"What is?" the Captain asked.

"Life is," the man replied.

"Did you come all the way up from the engine room to tell me that?" the Captain shouted. But just then he remembered he had asked the man to come up.

3

The sun seemed hardly to have moved when the Captain woke up. His first thought was of the passenger. He looked down at the dock. Except for a few gulls stirring uneasily in the wind or occasionally flapping their wings in aborted take-off, nothing moved. Maybe the passenger had arrived while he slept and seeing no one about, had returned to the office for a refund. Or perhaps after one look at the *Caspar*, he had decided on another means of travel to get to wherever he was going. One way or the other, there was nothing that could be done now but sail without him.

Yet, despite the Captain's earlier suspicion of trouble on the passage north, the passenger's failure to show up disturbed him. Maybe, he thought, Mueller, Miller, whatever his name was, had taken sick, or been in an accident, or had even been picked up by the police. Possibly O'Hare would know. He'd rest a bit longer, then call the office.

All that remained of his dream was the shadowy figure of the man from below claiming he had been asked to come, and a feeling of loneliness that had grown into a vague kind of terror.

The Captain closed his eyes and tried to recall what else had taken place in the dream. Only the figure remained, amorphous, isolated and unreal, a vision of eerie familiarity but with a thousand masks, one for every thought, every action, every desire. Probably, he reflected, dreams were some kind of valving mechanism to let off pressures of one kind or another. Or again, the aura of fear in the dream might well have been conceived out of vestiges of primordial fears of once real and life-threatening dangers, primitive fears long gone with the appearance of tools and weapons and the advent of civilized methods of mass security.

One way or the other, the Captain thought angrily, he'd like nothing better than a face to face confrontation with this illusive personality whose sole purpose seemed the creation of anxieties out of harmless events and capricious foreshadowings of dire things to come. He sighed dejectedly. Black thoughts in the bright light of the noonday sun.

A quick shadow passing over him interrupted his speculations. He looked up at Hoskins, his chief engineer, standing between him and the sun. His blue coveralls were streaked with grease but his hands and face looked recently washed.

"How is the engine?" the Captain asked.

"Be ready in a couple of hours, say about three," Hoskins replied pleasantly. "Them Whitneys are great old mills."

The Captain glanced at his watch, which showed twelve thirty-five.

"We'd like to knock off now," Hoskins said, "and get some chow."

"Go ahead," the Captain said. But as Hoskins turned to leave he called after him.

"You say the engine is all right?"

Hoskins paused and looked back. "The engine?" he repeated, staring into the Captain's face. "Why sure, it's in great shape. Them Whitneys never wear out."

"Well, that's a relief," the Captain thought and, sighing comfortably, drifted into his former languor. Hoskins' surprise at being asked twice about the engine caused him to chuckle softly. The old fellow didn't realize I was half asleep, he thought. Probably thinks I'm losing my mind. And that will worry him. He chuckled again. Great guy though, that Hoskins. And a good friend. Must be getting close to seventy himself. Came on in '14. No, 1915. World's Fair was on then. Let's see, that makes twenty years. Christ, twenty years here, twenty years there. God damn, all those years. They sure add up. Thirty, forty, fifty years. Psssst. Gone. Well, so they go and we grow old. And die. Good riddance to old garbage. Life is good, but once is enough, which is a lie, he thought bitterly. Life is good and there'll never be enough of it. But maybe the next ten years will go slower. There are ways of slowing up time, ways of manipulating it. Yes, ten good years, maybe even twenty up at Glen Ellen.

Glen Ellen in the Valley of the Moon. Who ever thought up such a saccharine name? But it was a pretty place. And his land was paid for long ago. In the hot sun, he could feel rather than see his five acres of fruit orchard and a cottage on the knoll. All was order, white picket fences, a bit of green lawn, flower beds and long lines of apricot and plum trees—squares, rectangles, parallel rows geometrically pleasing—all raked and tidy as it should be. On clear summer days he could look out from the veranda, with its profusion of purple bougainvillaea, and over the rolling hills of Sonoma, where live oaks daubed the yellow grasses and the ephemeral gray-green of olive groves lay here and there, lightly, like little smoke clouds at rest in the valley. Security? How often of late on dead cold ocean nights, at quarter speed off some fogbound coast, tense on the bridge with his senses straining against the hostile blackness, had the gentle warmth of Glen Ellen's sun-washed hills touched him with a loving hand. Safety. Ah yes, sweet nepenthe. The sailor's dream. Snug Harbor. God damn it. Euthanasia! And very soon, another trip or two, and he'd be retiring, leaving the sea, the great, restless sea, his sea that talked to him all day and all night in a thousand different voices. He'd be alone then in a painless purgatory, embalmed in blissful idleness. Something, he thought angrily, must be done about that, something to bring palpable reality into his paradise.

Suddenly a happy thought came to him. Emily Henderson! Instantly the whole picture, finished and framed, presented itself like a fine painting. And, like something wonderful, exciting and new that one suddenly finds oneself in possession of, to see and to have as one's own, his pulse began to beat more solidly. Why hadn't he thought of her before? Damn the reflective life, resigning oneself to reading, thinking, becoming the knowledgeable philosopher, forever striving to stop striving, building, stone by stone over the long years, a tomb in which to reflect upon life and all the while denying life itself, the full physical side, a woman's body.

He felt thirty years younger. He chuckled out loud. When old Hoskins hears about this, he'll be telling everyone "them Larsons never wear out." Yes, life is good, he thought, and sighing contentedly, pulled his cap down over his eyes and prepared himself for another short nap in the sun.

The high-pitched crying of gulls in startled flight roused him. From the dock came the rumble of tires over wooden planks. A car door slammed. Mingled with the whine of the wind he could hear a motor running. The Captain yawned, stretched, then rose reluctantly from his chair and walked to the rail.

An ancient taxicab stood at the end of the warehouse. By the heavy chugging of the engine, the high, thin-tired wheels, the dull nondescript paint on the body, the Captain guessed it to be at least twenty years old. A man got out, paid the driver and started toward the gangway. In one hand he carried a black briefcase, over his other arm a dark topcoat. At the foot of the gangway he hesitated and looked up at the *Caspar*. The hot, dusty wind, sweeping across the dock, flapped the loose ends of the straps on his briefcase, lifted the collar of his suit coat up around his neck. The Captain, apprehensive and at once deeply curious, directed him to the forequarter.

Sweat was running down the man's face when he set his briefcase on the deck. He took a white handkerchief from the breast pocket of his dark, double-breasted business suit, removed his gray felt hat and wiped his face. On the dock, the Captain had judged him to be in his late fifties. On closer inspection, however, he appeared much older. How much, the Captain could not tell. He was gray-haired and thin with an angular face, a wide thin mouth and prominent cheek bones. His deep-set eyes moved restlessly, seeming to take in every detail with quick appraisal. He was quite pale and there was a nervous tightening of the skin about his eyes. He looked up at the stack then down at the gulls facing into the wind on the dock. Finally, his restless gaze paused as it met the Captain's. And in that moment, a tiny current of recognition was generated in the Captain's mind. But whether or not the passenger experienced a similar response, he showed no sign.

"My name is Mueller," the passenger said, "William Mueller." His voice, though barely above a whisper, was clearly audible.

"I'm Captain Larson. Your cabin is right over there." The Captain pointed toward the small stateroom he'd made ready that morning. "It'll be hot in there, but it'll cool off as soon as we leave the channel."

"I do not mind the heat," Mueller said. He spoke with a slight trace of an accent, possibly Scandinavian, but with precision, as though he had acquired the language by careful study. After picking up his briefcase, he hurried to the cabin, stepped inside and closed the door behind him. A moment later the Captain heard the port snap shut and the toggle screw click against the brass frame.

The Captain returned to his deck chair, but Mueller did not come out. He waited awhile thinking that perhaps Mueller might change from his business suit into something more comfortable and get out of the stuffy cabin. Still he did not come out. Nor did he open the port.

There was no change at all in the wind. Through the black trusses of the drawbridge astern, the Captain could see the blue expanse of bay stippled with whitecaps, and all of it, like a great dark river, crawled steadily southward. He could not recall having seen the sky so clear. He picked up the *Collected Works of Dostoevsky* and turned to *Notes From the Underground.* But the provocative lines he'd underscored only a short while before, which had so absorbed his attention, seemed completely irrelevant and without purpose. He could think of nothing but the passenger.

Where had he come from? Why had he chosen such an antiquated and uncomfortable mode of travel when he could just as easily have taken a train or even a bus? Why did he have that odd feeling of having seen him before when there was no one in all his life he could remember who bore even a faint resemblance to the pallid nervousness of the man now occupying the passenger's cabin? A peculiarly urgent desire to know more about him possessed the Captain, a desire that was tinged with mistrust and a vague sense of fear. He lay back on his deck chair and, with the now unreadable Dostoevsky open before him, began to lay tentative plans on how he would approach this stranger, tactfully, cautiously to be sure, to draw him out.

A big gray gull, tired of fighting the upper currents, swung down over the deck, screamed shrilly and swooped away over the channel. With his thoughts still taken up with the passenger, the Captain closed his eyes. A deep and unexplainable weariness came over him. How strange, he thought, that he should be so sleepy at that time of day. As far back as he could remember, he had avoided sleep, often reading until early morning or just fussing around doing little things to keep from turning in. Now, though he much preferred to stay awake, if for no other reason than to amuse himself with these errant thoughts of his, his body, warm and relaxed in the sun, could not be coerced. Nor could his brain. So once again that afternoon, he drifted off into a light but restless sleep through which filtered a steady flow of oddly familiar faces and essences of old and half forgotten experiences.

And through it all, now near, now far, came the low sound of sobbing that, except for intermittent breaks as after quick exhalations, could have been the atonal sighing of the north wind through the rigging.

A slight sound, or perhaps it was an awareness of some unusual presence close by, awakened him. He yawned, brushed a weathered hand across his mouth and opened his eyes. To his surprise, Mueller was sitting in a deck chair beside him. He was dressed in the same dark, double-breasted suit with his gray felt hat pulled down over his eyes very much like the Captain's. But Mueller was wide awake, gazing down at the deck in front of him. How long he'd been there, the Captain had no way of knowing. Yet, by the position of the sun, which the Captain noted was standing at about the same angle, very little time must have passed.

"You were sleeping," Mueller said in his clear whisper. "I did not wish to disturb you."

"It's not my habit to sleep in the afternoon," the Captain said gruffly to cover the embarrassment of what he was certain must appear as grossly unseamanlike behavior to this stranger aboard. "The combination of hot sun," he went on apologetically, "and this damned north wind must have gotten to me."

"It was very close in the cabin," Mueller said, unmindful of the Captain's apology. "I thought we might talk awhile out here."

The lines of tension about his eyes were more pronounced and he seemed to the Captain to have aged considerably in the brief time since he had come aboard. He looked anxious, as though time were running out. Again a feeling came over the Captain of having seen him before. He scrutinized Mueller's features carefully, but as a result of the glare of sunlight, or from a slight dizziness that had come over him on waking, both the face and the figure in the adjoining chair seemed blurred and darkened. Perhaps, he thought, it was merely Mueller's clear, whispery voice with its overtone of worldly sadness that stirred his feeling of recognition. Yet whether he had met the passenger at some previous but forgotten time, or whether he was a total stranger, concerned him less at the moment than where he might be bound.

"What made you take the *Caspar* on your trip north?" the Captain asked.

"An impulse," Mueller said. "An impulse with no thought whatever." He paused as if considering whether or not to go on. "I'd been walking all night," he said, finally. "It's a good feeling to walk through the streets at night. There is always the chance that something might happen. Also one takes a certain risk."

"A considerable risk, I'd say," the Captain interjected. "But how did you happen on to the *Caspar*?"

"As I said, I was walking, from the hills down toward the bay. Not a straight course, mind you, but erratic and unpredictable. My life has always been that way, like those planets the old astronomers called the Wanderers. A strong wind was blowing and the sky was clear. Above me, and somewhat to the north, stood the Seven Stars of Ursa which the ancient Pythagoreans called the Hands of Rhea, the Lady of Turning Heaven. Scattered about like a collage of early Greek family portraits and concealing the deeper blackness beyond, I could make out Andromeda, Cassiopea, Cepheus, Perseus, and then the dimly perceived swath of the galaxy, the Bridge Out of Time.

"Yet though the sky was filled with action, the city was quite dark in spite of the street lamps and the stars. I probably covered a dozen miles walking this way and that, through alleys and little parks and along deserted streets. Yes, action and all those stars!" Mueller turned his shadowed face toward the Captain. "But there was nothing," he added slowly.

"Nothing?" the Captain repeated. "What were you looking for?"

"Change," Mueller said quickly, as if he had anticipated the question. "Change like a narcotic bringing temporary forgetfulness." He paused again and breathed in softly. "Of course," he said, "you know what I mean."

"I'm not sure I follow you," the Captain murmured, probing the indistinct features of the man next to him from the shade of his visor, and wondering what he should do if this passenger of his should prove to be what he was beginning to suspect, some kind of psychopath.

"I have a theory," Mueller went on, "that all of us, the most rational and hard-headed of men as well as the softest and most malleable, the pious believers as well as the dedicated practitioners of the responsible life, share a common fear which is either active or passive but always there like one's heartbeat or . . ."

"You were walking about in the middle of the night," the Captain interrupted impatiently. "How did you stumble onto the *Caspar*?"

"That came later," Mueller said, undisturbed by the Captain's intrusion. "I thought you would understand."

"Understand!" the Captain muttered. What goes on with this man with his "of course you know what I mean" and now his "I thought you would understand"? Is he sane or some kind of crackpot? And what is he doing aboard this nearly defunct lumber schooner dressed up like an A-deck passenger on a Pacific liner? Maybe he's an insurance investigator or possibly a government agent and has mistaken me for someone else. He might even be an escapee from some mental asylum! But whoever he is, he'll be here for a whole week and I'll have to put up with him. Well, at least he doesn't seem dangerous.

No, there was certainly nothing dangerous about Mueller, the Captain reflected, nothing at all vicious, nor even malicious. He'd had enough experience to judge that. In fact, he thought, there was something rather pathetic about him. Perhaps he shouldn't have been so abrupt with him. He looked again at Mueller. Only his eyes, set in hollows of deepest shadow and looking back at him as though from a long way off or through a great distance of time, were visible.

Whether the expression of tragic resignation in Mueller's eyes mixed with the enduring pain of some very old injury was due to the blurring of the Captain's vision or whether, as he was beginning to suspect, it was the projection of some concealed trouble of his own being mirrored back to him, he could not tell. But it was at that moment he felt again the same feeling of recognition as before, only stronger now, like a dark wind out of his past, but for which he could find no support whatever from his conscious recollections.

"I'm sorry for the interruption," the Captain said. "As I said, it's probably that damned sun and the wind up there blowing a gale that's making me a bit irritable."

"Feelings are unruly and have a way of transgressing upon order as we would like to have it," Mueller said.

"Perhaps that's true," the Captain said, though he was not in the least sure what Mueller meant. "But tell me," he asked, "who are you and why have you taken passage on the *Caspar*?"

Mueller was silent, dead silent in his dark retreat. Finally his shadowed gaze turned slowly upon the Captain.

"I thought by now you would surely know," he replied.

The Captain sighed and rubbed his eyes. "I haven't the slightest idea who you are," he said wearily.

"But it was you who wanted me to come," Mueller said.

4

In spite of the Captain's increasing suspicion concerning Mueller's sanity, this last statement so unnerved him that momentarily he could think of nothing but to wish for old Hoskins, with his homely chatter, to appear and reestablish his contact with reality, which in Mueller's presence was fast taking on the aspects of a distressing dream.

But Hoskins was nowhere about. And there was no sound from below. Certainly, the Captain thought, Hoskins and the men must have long since returned from lunch. Or perhaps they had returned while he slept, finished their work on the engine, and gone off again. He glanced at the sky. The sun, with its lower limb just above the black, tarred mizzen shrouds, seemed fixed at a permanent angle. No smoke came from the stack. In fact, there was no motion of any kind except the very slight oscillation of the mastheads against the sky and the almost visual surge of the wind above. The engine could have been repaired, run for awhile, then shut down. On the other hand, the men could still be at lunch. The smokeless stack and the silence told him nothing. He wondered about the time but somehow lacked the energy to look at his watch, which he could hear ticking away in its gold-plated case in the vest pocket of his uniform.

He turned again to Mueller hoping that by some magic he would have vanished, or that he had never been there in the first place. But the dark figure of the passenger remained as before, indistinct and motionless, like the shadow of a man, leaning slightly forward on his white canvas deck chair. He was still talking, and in the same low whisper.

"I've come a long way, from the ends of the earth, you might say. But the most distant places do not seem very far once you have been there and returned."

"I wouldn't know about that," the Captain murmured, at a loss how to respond to these perplexingly elusive statements, which on the surface seemed meaningless, yet somehow imparted a feeling of motion toward some distant and nebulous goal. Perhaps Mueller was trying to tell him something!

In spite of the burning sun, the Captain felt cold inside. Was Mueller an hallucination, he wondered, the distorted product of some breakdown in his overtired mental machinery, or was he, as he was beginning to fear, the visitation of Death? Probably neither, he consoled himself. Though he was unusually tired, his mind was as clear as ever. And Death, at least in human form, he knew was a gross superstition. Moreover, Death, as he understood it from popular mythology, was impassive, taciturn and silently adamant. Mueller, though cryptic, was uniquely verbal. And despite his lack of logical continuity, he seemed possessed of profound feelings that seemed to rise, like random bubbles from the darkest chambers of his being, feelings as well as insights charged with hidden meanings but entirely devoid of laughter and love, and remarkably like those of a troubled dream. It was as if Mueller's assessment of reality had been conceived in the subterranean gloom of the Captain's own mind.

The thought stirred the same hollow feeling that had come over him after his dream of the mysterious black figure from the depths of the engine room.

"It's a difficult habit to break."

"What is?"

"Life is."

In Mueller's presence, faceless as a dream persona, elucidating in his eerie whisper dark and ineluctable truths fomented in primitive regions beyond the pale of sunlight and blue sky, the Captain sensed with foreboding the advent of a confrontation far worse than his own demise.

But what could Mueller possibly have to say? His whole life was clean. He had wronged no one. In fact, for the most part, it had been rather dull, fearing nothing really, and as far as he knew, feared by no one. Or was it all, he wondered, some weird kind of joke being played on him by some old shipmate with a macabre sense of humor? If so, to hell with him and his bastard accomplice. Yet, no matter how he reasoned, he could not rid himself of the unpleasant feeling of being drawn in.

"Travel comes from travail, to suffer, and travail derives from trepalium, an instrument of torture. When one willfully seeks suffering for its own sake, it is usually a last desperate grasp for reality."

Now what could he mean by all that, travel, travail, trepalium? Mueller himself was a trepalium, an insidious instrument of torture! What worse pain could one inflict upon a man than to pin him down and pour this black gibberish into his ears?

Well, there was one thing this audacious passenger of his had not reckoned with, the authority of a ship's master. He would have him thrown off the *Caspar* immediately. He'd do it himself, by God! And to hell with the agent or the general manager or the whole damn company, for that matter. He'd put in too many years of faithful service, of miserable, body breaking labor, to be forced to listen to Mueller's mad ramblings. Goaded by angry indignation, he started to rise from his chair. He would stand up to his full height, which he judged to be about equal to Mueller's, point to the gangway and order this lunatic off his ship.

He could not move. All coordination had left him. His muscles refused, absolutely, to respond to his will. Even his hands, accustomed for half a century to handling heavy gear, were powerless to grip the wooden armrest of the deck chair. Desperation and then panic seized him.

What had happened to him? Exhaustion? Too much direct sunlight? The dry, hyperborean wind and a high barometer? Or was Mueller's whisper, which seemed to rise like an invocation from the depths of the Captain's unconscious, exercising some mysterious control over his mental processes?

Just then, a series of distinctly disagreeable questions intruded into his mind. Could this paralysis of his, he wondered, weaken his hard-won resistance to the metaphysical terrors of his childhood just as deep sleep had weakened his defenses against the dream depredations of the grease-blackened workman from below? And would his incapacity soften him up for the frontal attack he sensed Mueller had been preparing for him since the moment he came aboard?

One way or another, he could still speak, think and defend himself with his reason. Besides, this whole ridiculous situation would soon pass, he felt certain. It would have to pass. There was work to be done.

None of the turmoil that wracked the Captain's mind and body seemed to affect Mueller in the least. Or, if it did, he showed no sign by any change in his voice, or in the steady flow of words that followed with the persistence of the shadow that he, himself, appeared to be.

"It was the ticking of a clock that sent me on this journey that has no end," he said. "Think of that, an old wall-hung clock, its oak frame darkened by time to a dull black and its heavy pendulum swinging impassively in obedience to a law, Galileo's, to be exact, but in reality, immune to all laws, a mere mechanical device designed to calibrate the flow of time. As though time were a river with a source and a destination! Think of it, wheels geared to pointers that attempt to divide nothingness into finite and palpable parts. Lying in bed at six or seven or eight years old, I could hear, from the dark outer hall, the light tick, as the pendulum swept with infinite leisure through its arc, tripped the escapement wheel, and then the dull tock of the blocked cog on the return journey. Nightlong footsteps going nowhere. Don't you agree that it is madness, the hope only of desperate men, to attempt to harness and measure nothingness?"

"Agree?" the Captain asked. His voice was weak but his fear had ebbed somewhat as he resigned himself to Mueller's unrelenting discourse. "At the moment, I do not know what to think, but it would seem to me that only some sort of insanity would cause a man to take such a peculiar view of something as ordinary as a grandfather clock hanging on the wall outside his bedroom."

"Have you never listened to a clock then," Mueller asked, "and counted each tick, yet knowing, as you lay in the dark, that there would always be more ticks, in numbers without end, that you could count until the clock stopped, until all the clocks stopped, and still go on counting, and that the whole thing was meaningless?"

"I had better things to think about," the Captain replied, feeling increasingly more at ease as he became aware that the mystery of Mueller's behavior lay in some deep well of internal disturbance and that he meant no harm. Obsessed by some problem or other, the news of an illness perhaps, a death, the rupture of some old psychic wound, or by any one of the "ten thousand troubles" which, according to the ancient Chinese, made up a man's life, Mueller had probably rushed out into the night, and after wandering through the streets till daybreak, had stumbled upon the company's dock office, and as he had said, impulsively booked passage on the first ship out. However, now that he had found a listener, albeit an unwilling one, he would no doubt pour out the tale of his misery, elaborating each detail and dwelling with brutal self-interest upon the scope and the magnitude of his suffering.

The Captain sighed deeply. How many tales of a similar nature had he heard in the past? And yet not once, as far as he could remember, had he himself sought help from another. He sighed again and tried to lift his hand to wipe a trickle of sweat from his forehead. His hand felt far away as though it belonged to another body. A temporary loss of circulation, he thought, and felt no special concern. On the adjoining armrest he could see the pale hand of the passenger. The bony fingers lying limply on the sun-bleached wood looked remarkably like his own. Yes, he reflected, he'd had a fairly trouble-free time of it, moments of danger to be sure, and pain not to be forgotten, but nothing covering him like the miserable wretch beside him.

"So we arrive by night at a strange crossing," Mueller was saying, " . . . which road we take is not a matter of choice, for there is no choice between two unfamiliar identicals. At such a moment we are at the mercy of fate. You, with no pre-knowledge whatever, turn right and shortly find a refuge from the hostile night, while I, in equal ignorance, but seeking the same end, go to the left and disappear into nothingness."

"Which road indeed!" the Captain mumbled irritably. Just then, and for no reason at all, a scene flashed before his mind—a cross upon which hung a dark Christ on a backdrop of intense blackness. But the expression on the exhausted face was not the familiar one of universal sorrow. The distorted features, mouth twisted, eyes rolled upward under netted lines of violent stress, transmitted so vividly the terror of total abandonment to an abyss of nothingness, and with such a complete communication of terror, it seemed to the Captain that, for an instant, he was a witness to his own crucifixion and his precipitation into the nothingness on the dark side of infinity.

The scene vanished quickly, and oddly enough, though the experience had no precedent, he felt no surprise. Could all he had known about that, he wondered, long discarded but emotionally sustained, have been a huge dissimulation, or at the least, an unintended misinterpretation?

But what had all this to do with Mueller's crossroads? And what about his clock? Was there some direction, after all, to his incomprehensible digressions? If so, where was he heading, this shadowy being with his whispery voice and his random soliloquies that could stir up the dregs in the time-deep bottoms of feeling?

"Between the before and the after there is a crucial pause, a moment of silent hesitation as the pendulum begins its swing either to the right or to the left. I can remember the before like a bright summer day that extended back beyond memory, which is to say, in effect, it had no beginning. No time flowed by the before. It was a tranquil island in a tideless sea. Then somewhere, somehow, an awareness crept in like a shadow without a source. What followed after was a long and progressively deepening darkness. And once you have fully experienced darkness there can never be light again."

As usual, a pause followed this singular disclosure during which the Captain could hear the sound of a match being struck, followed by the familiar and acrid smell of Hoskins' cigar smoke.

"We should have talked long ago," Mueller went on. His voice, though still in a whisper, had grown more confidential as though some barrier between them had been parted. "We should have come to know one another. Our problem may not have been resolved, but with the two of us together, it might have been more tolerable." He did not stop. "The first six years was an island cut off entirely from every kind of fear except that induced by childish fancy to stimulate and further incite the imagination, and anticipation, of dream creation, of simple, sensual satisfactions. It was a long, slow, indrawing of a breath before the plunge.

"And then one winter afternoon, coming home from school, I was stopped by a neighbor lady with teary eyes and little suffocated sobs, and again by my father with two deadly quiet words, 'Mother's dead.'

"Well now, that meant nothing to me. I felt nothing one way or another. I was frightened only by the fear and the sorrow of those who had told me. If the neighbor lady had said, 'William, you lucky boy, your mother is dead,' and laughed with joy, I might have laughed too. And if my father had flipped me a nickel and said, 'Go buy yourself a bag of candy, your mother's dead,' I would, no doubt, have run off to the grocery store, happy and unconcerned.

"I went to my room upstairs at the end of the hall as I was told, washed my hands and face in the old marble-topped basin in the alcove beside my bed, combed my hair with a nice straight part down the middle, changed into my Sunday clothes, and buttoned up my good patent leather shoes. Then I sat on my bed and fiddled with the brass caps on the white iron bedstead until my father should call me down to the parlor where I had a feeling my mother would be. As I twisted the caps and ran my fingers across the iron rungs, I felt nothing but irritation for having been made to dress up in my best clothes when I could have been playing outside on the sidewalk with my coaster until dark.

"Except for the noise I made with the bedstead, the only sound in my room came from the ticking of the big clock in the hall which, because it had hung there ticking away since before I was born, I was no longer conscious of. After awhile my father entered, took me by the hand, and led me down to the parlor where my mother, looking quite nice with her dark brown hair done up and her hands folded over her breast, lay with her eyes closed in a white casket which stood on a pedestal, with a velvet drape hanging to the floor.

"I wanted to go outside. It was getting dark, but I wanted to go outside anyway and play on the sidewalk. Of course I didn't ask my father if I could go. He looked so strange, like someone I didn't know standing by the head of the casket with his face like night. Yet his eyes were shining in the light of the tall flames from the candelabra that was only lit on Christmas Eve. So I just stood there, a little way back and stared at them both, my dark, quiet father and my mother's white face that had not moved once.

"I knew she was dead. I had been told that twice, and I could see from the white box in which she lay and the long time that she didn't move, that she really was dead. And I knew I should be crying, that it was expected of me. But I didn't feel like crying. Besides, I was getting hungry and wanted to get out of the dark parlor with its candlelight and shadows and into the bright gaslight in the kitchen and get at the dinner I knew my mother would have cooking on the big, black coal-burning stove, where it would be warm and cozy and we could laugh while we ate and maybe sing a song or two before I went up to do my homework.

"But we went out to eat, or rather, we went out so I could eat, because my father wanted nothing. We went to the neighbor lady's house where I was served corned beef and cabbage and boiled potatoes. I ate everything except the mustard, which was the hot kind, and the horse radish. And all the while I was eating, the old neighbor lady patted my head, and in between sobs and snuffles, kept asking my father how in the world he would ever manage a six-year-old boy by himself.

"When I finished the apple cobbler I got sleepy, and my father, with never a word, took me by the hand and we walked up the steep sidewalk, past the two gas lamps and across the cobblestone street until we came to our house, with its narrow bay windows, looking very still except for the guttering of low-burning candles in the parlor.

"I got into my nightgown, said a quick prayer on my knees by the bed, asking God to bless Mother and Father, then I curled up under the soft patchwork quilt my mother had sewn on since before I could remember. After being kissed on both cheeks very gently by my father, I went to sleep.

"It was the clock that woke me, the same old clock that had ticked away in the hallway outside my bedroom all the days of my life, but which I never really heard.

"I woke up thinking, as though my thoughts were a busy road that wound up out of the depths of my mind. I thought about the hearse rocking over the cobblestones through the early fog. I could even see the pale sprouts of winter grass being crushed under the hard rubber tires and the horses stumbling and slipping on the steep hill. I sat up in my bed and looked out the window. The sky was black and the city too, except for the street lights, very small and quiet, following diverging paths over the wide slopes and valleys and away to some unpleasantly unfamiliar rim of deeper darkness. And as I looked through the window, it seemed those still little points were long lines of pale dead stars tracking the surface of immense waves of blackness.

"The ticking of the clock was loud and so clear I could hear the click of the escapement wheel and even, I thought, the rotation of the gears. It was like I was seeing it all under a huge magnifying glass. The sound of it filled the room with harsh throbbing which echoed down the empty hallway.

"And still my thoughts went on, following one after another like a night train of silent coaches. I saw every detail of the long, slow journey to the graveyard, the sealed casket with its wreathes of heavy-smelling flowers and narrow, black, velvet-covered seats on either side in the rear with my father on one side, his black hat in his lap, and Aunt Hilda and Cousin Ilsa opposite, staring straight in front of them. It seemed as though I had experienced it all before. There was even an incident. When the driver whipped up the horses to make the last steep pull up the hill through the open gates of the graveyard, the hearse lurched to one side and the casket slipped back down the aisle. My father leaped forward, his face gray and tight, and, clinging to one of the ebony handholds as if to stop the heavy casket from going through the door, let out a high, thin cry.

"And all the while these pictures passed before my mind, the clock kept up its steady beat, filling the room, as I said, and echoing in the hallway with its brash, metallic ticking. I didn't visualize the lowering of the casket into the grave. I fell asleep again. When I woke up it was late afternoon. I could tell that by the winter shadows on the floor. I was lying on my left side and I could feel my heart beating. It was exactly in phase with the ticking of the clock in the hall. The old neighbor lady, dressed all in black, was standing beside my bed. She was rubbing my hands and arms and making little whimpering noises. Nearby on a small stand was some broth in a white bowl that did not belong to our house. Just then I realized the clock had stopped."

5

High in the crosstrees, the wind continued its low whimpering cry, changing from time to time to a series of short little gasps. The hot sun burned down steadily from its still slightly westward inclination. At any time now, the Captain thought, Hoskins would be making his appearance. Perhaps he should not be lying there wasting time in a futile attempt to grasp the significance of Mueller's arcane ramblings.

Residual guilt, stirred by the knowledge of work to be done, or fear of doing nothing, forced a sigh of concern. Work and action, the aegis of his life. A protective screen? Protection from what? A question indeed. No doubt Mueller would come up with some murky answer. Was this his mission then, to seek out a kindred soul in that city of over half a million disparate personalities for the single purpose of revealing a mystery that in all probability did not exist? Kindred soul! What kinship had he with Mueller? He shared nothing at all with this fear-haunted, shadow-of-a-man, the distorted lens of his mind's eye infusing the simple reality of things with weird significance and strange dimensions while his own consistently practical mind, even since an early age, had been happy with conditions as he had found them. So there was an attempt to escape into the temporary sanctuary of forgetfulness. But a kind old lady had brought him back. No, it was the clock that had brought him back. But the clock had stopped. Yes, of course.

"Have you never listened to a clock then?" Mueller's question came back to him.

I had better things to do, the Captain thought. Yet since Mueller had brought it up, he did remember a clock in the old house where he was born, a fine Seth Thomas with a porcelain face and bronze Roman numerals. The clock belonged to his father, Captain Lars Larson, retired master of sail and steam, and then, as befitted an aging mariner, a San Francisco bar pilot. The clock was his father's pleasure and his responsibility. He unlocked it every Sunday morning before church and wound it slowly, methodically, with a brass key of a quaint antique design. Yet it was a clock. Nothing more. And certainly not Mueller's dread symbol of time without end.

Vividly, happily—not at all like the somber passage of anomalous visions on the shifting screens of Mueller's memory—he could see his room at the end of the hall with its high-coved ceiling above an embossed plaster moulding. At the center of the ceiling and directly above his bed a gas chandelier was suspended from three chains that met in a medallion of gold vine leaves—the repository of his hedonistic dreams. All manner of adventures took place deep in that golden foliage. Often there appeared a young girl of surpassing beauty.

But what would Mueller know of all this, picnics in the park, ferry boat rides, the view from his bedroom window that faced west to where the late afternoon fog in a vast silver wave engulfed the hills and licked at the city with curling tongues of mist? And the toys that grew in size from bathtub steamboats and miniature warships to a full-fledged sailing dory with clear, white cedar planking, a dagger board and a mahogany tiller with a Turk's head knot? And what would Mueller do with such a luxury? Explore the waterfront? Sail right under the high sterns of ocean going square-riggers and gaze up at their huge rudders and iron bark rudderposts? Would he wonder at the mighty transoms carved with exotic names and home ports like Haakon I, Bergen; Arminius, Hamburg; Reina Isabella, Barcellona; Orion, Liverpool? Would he dare sail out to Goat Island, beach his craft in a sandy cove and climb through thick brush to the crest of the mountain and gaze, like a pirate, at the city through his polished brass long glass?

Was all this not enough, he wondered, to light a small fire in the wintery soul of his dour companion? Though Mueller was no longer visible, his presence remained like a potential danger lurking on the shadowy verge of his memory. Was he asleep in the hot sun? Or was he ruminating on more of his disheartening thoughts?

"An andabata was a Roman gladiator who fought mounted wearing a helmet without eyeslits," Mueller whispered.

"All that is ancient history," the Captain said, impatiently. "Another time and another culture. So what's the point in bringing it up?"

"He could not see his enemy."

"What enemy?" the Captain asked.

Since Mueller did not answer, the Captain returned to his recollections. With his eyes still closed he beheld, in three dimensions, his teak desk salvaged from a German barkentine that had gone on the rocks at Fort Point, Burma teak hauled by elephants with chains out of the rain forests of Mandalay and rafted down the Irrawaddy River, his father said. Smooth, fine-grained teak with coat after coat of glossy, hard tung oil varnish that reflected his face in its honey dark depths. Clear autumn nights, light southwest breezes whispering in the eaves and homework at his teakwood desk, the omphalos, the center of his universe, birthplace of knowledge, geography, history, compositions, literature, mathematics and dreams in the yellow glow of the kerosene lantern.

And his books! Jules Verne's *Twenty Thousand Leagues Under the Sea*; Melville's *Moby-Dick*, *Typee* and *Omoo*; Nathaniel Bowditch's *The American Practical Navigator*; and the stained and broken-backed volume of *Madame Bovary* kept hidden in a drawer. Those were the bright times, of preparation for his voyages of discovery, his quest of the Grail. Bowditch was his armor and sword. Sun time, star time, hour angles, right ascension, declination, azimuth, fabulous words, like the crown and scepter, symbolizing the power and the glory. Mathematics was its essence. A knowledge of mathematics separates the deck hands from the officers, his father said. It is the queen of the sciences. But for him it was more. It was an adventure into abstraction with no guidance but the rules of the game. So what mattered the lateness of the hour when a problem was to be solved, an equation learned. To be too conscious was no illness, he reflected, it was a joy.

What more could a boy want? And what more could Mueller say, the Captain wondered. There was no refutation, no gloom to be cast over those happy reminiscences. Yet he was certain that Mueller would come up with something. Whoever or whatever he was, he was anathema, a paradigm of pessimism, the negation of life. The essence of Mueller was non-being.

No matter, the Captain concluded, he would soon be free of his disturbing intrusions. Before long the crew would be back, the lines cast off and the *Caspar* would be on her way North to Eureka and beyond. Once through the Gate, he'd take the North Channel past Point Bonita. With a land wind blowing, the sea would be calm in the lee of the mountains. By evening, the wind would be gone, the air clear, and the night sky awash with stars from horizon to horizon.

6

Except for the soughing aloft, not a sound could be heard either on the ship or on the dock. Nor from the deck chair beside him. Maybe Mueller had finally grown tired of talking and had actually gone to sleep. Or, and this was almost too much to hope for, this querulous passenger of his would turn out to be a figment of his imagination, an unconscious anxiety manifesting itself in the form of some melancholic doppelganger.

"Some mysteries are best left unsolved."

It was Mueller again, and by the ominously low pitch in his whispery voice, it was obvious more would follow, a chilling epilogue, no doubt, the Captain thought glumly, to the happy memories of his youth.

"Fabulous dreams are often close companions of fabulous fears, which they either complement or destroy."

"Destroy what?" the Captain asked, trying to conceal his agitation.

"The fears that provide the vitality of ambition and of life itself."

Now how could anyone possibly respond to such absurd assertions, the Captain wondered, angrily. Yet he felt compelled to say something, if only to refute Mueller's arrogant certitudes.

"You do not mention faith, which transcends all fears and clears the path to fulfillment."

"Faith is the shield of the fearful. It can protect one from the fear of death," Mueller conceded, "but not of terror unbridled, of fading forever and never dying."

"Faith is so tightly bound up with the mysterious vacillations of feeling," the Captain rushed on, "that no amount of reason can alter it once it has taken root, nor discourage its growth, nor plant the seed of a new faith."

He paused to consider his statement, its scope and significance, then realized that he had either lost his thread of thought or that he had had none to begin with.

"I once had a book," Mueller said, "a slender, pale green volume that, in my innocence, I felt certain held the key to the secret of the universe. Neither the Bible, the great works of philosophy, nor the wisdom of the sages engendered in me such glorious hope."

"And the book?" the Captain asked, apprehensively.

"*Hartman's Elements of Analytic Geometry.*"

"Hope in geometry?"

"Not only hope, but the entire gamut of emotional experience from pleasure to terror."

"Pleasure, yes. Hope, conceivably. But terror?"

"You, of all people, must know that to be born with a reasoning mind is reason enough to know terror all the days of one's life."

"To be too conscious . . . ," the Captain began, hesitated, then withdrew into silence. Yet though his mind was clear and his senses alert to the undiminished whine of the wind, and even to the sound of retreating footsteps across the deck, he was powerless to stop what he intuited Mueller was about to tell him.

"Had it not been for my father," Mueller began, "I would have left school and wandered about. I would have taken odd jobs in the fields, in the factories, in the gold mines. I would have written simple poetry, expressed my nature. But there was my father, a tired little man, pottering in his garden, dreaming perhaps of the high days of his youth and waiting for me to perpetuate his waning life.

"I plunged deeper into my studies. The night stars I saw no more and only a little of the sun. Then one night I was working. A simple problem. An asymptote, a line sweeping down in a beautiful curve to meet the x-axis at infinity. The solution of the problem was infinity. There, I marked it so with the sign of infinity, the eight on its side. Tired, I looked at the symbol and retraced it with my pencil. It was a simple problem, the answer was infinity. No. It had two answers. I marked the coordinates, laid in a line approaching the y-axis. A beautiful curve sweeping up to infinity. Infinity on both ends. I marked it so with the sign of infinity, the eight on its side. I retraced the sign with my pencil. It grew deeper and blacker. It was a simple problem. The answer was infinity on both ends.

"Outside my window I heard the whispering of the sea wind, low in its tone as the voice of one who has come far and is weary.

"The problem was solved. It was clearly intelligible, set down in an equation, the coordinates marked, the curve drawn in. The answer was infinity both ways. How far to infinity? A long way, a weary way. And then what? Nothing perhaps, only infinity again. An endless journey growing smaller, whispering away into nothingness.

"Pallid moonbeams, slanting through trembling black leaves, lighted the bare walls of my room above the shaded lamp. A cold light, polarized light, electromagnetic waves vibrating in but one plane, cast off light from the sun, but still a cold light. And the answer was infinity. It held, for there was no meeting of the lines, only in that one place which was no place.

"The pine branches rustled. The sea wind murmured in the autumn night, whispering low and hollow as it slipped

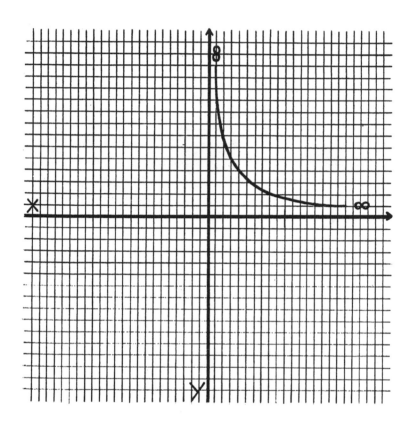

away over the hills into the darkness. An endless journey, on and away, sweeping down the curve to infinity.

"But there were two answers, the beginning and the end. Two curves joined in the fullness of the moment. The upswing of the wind's dark emergence from the sea. A fleeting passage, movement and a voice under the clear night sky, sad in its tone, the sadness of despair. Then onward into the endless night.

"Slowly, as slowly as time bearing the weight of the universe, my mind received the image of the thing that was nothing. Cold, vague, beyond dimension, flowing as the wind flows. The mind that had reached for the substance found only the shadow. And the shadow was nothing, only the absence, unseen by the eyes, but appearing.

"The lamp cast its short cone of whiteness in a circle on the paper. There the lines were clear and black, the equation set down in formulated order, the conclusion, ultimate, absolute, unvariable, the end of the end, the end of all things, $x = \text{ffi}$, $y = \text{ffi}$. And the curve on the paper, like the sun, a moment of light bound by darkness, born to flame, to burn out, finally to become a dark star clinging to its orbital track, or to fall away and drift in the void, alone with the winds of space.

"Outside, the wind whimpered like an endless dying. It breathed the chill of late night through the half open window. I turned out the light. The moon had set, the room dissolved in darkness. I was alone with the wind. Slowly, the image that had formed crept deeper into my mind to flow like a downward coldness into my chest, a paralyzing flux that spread through all my body.

"For a moment I was held by the magnitude of a fear that passed beyond the verge of time and space, crushed down with suffocating closeness in timeless, drifting wind, aware only of the ether hum of eternity. I closed the window and pulled the shade. I flung the heavy drapes across. Then I fell back in my chair exhausted and listened to the beating of my heart."

Though the Captain could no longer feel the heat from the sun, nor hear the whistling of the north wind above him, his mind had grown suddenly lucid. "It seems to me," he said, "that you were not seeking pleasure in the abstractions of mathematics as much as an escape into self-forgetfulness. But once the problem was solved and the answer set down in formulated order, a new and much greater problem arose proving that self-forgetfulness is no impregnable asylum."

"Between every action and every thought there is a perilous moment," Mueller said, "in which the abiding consciousness of one's essential nothingness rushes in like a cold wind from infinite space. To extinguish the intervals of nullity and keep running is the game of life."

7

CAPTAIN: "The third noble truth proclaims the release from sorrow is by the extinction of the ego with its desire for pleasure, its sense of duty, and its fear of death."

MUELLER: "There is only one release from ego. All others are self-deceptions."

CAPTAIN (sighing): "So familiar. I once knew someone who looked like you, thought like you, spoke like you. Somewhere, I'm sure."

MUELLER: "I have a common face so I wear no mask. Therefore, everyone sees in me someone they once knew but can't quite remember. They're troubled. They think of me between times. They search their memories. Still they'd rather I be masked."

CAPTAIN: "The fruit from the tree of knowledge is sometimes bitter. Truth is bitter."

MUELLER: "There is no truth. One man's truth is another man's fable."

CAPTAIN: "There is faith."

MUELLER: "The dead end of hope."

CAPTAIN: "I have known honorable men. I have practiced honesty."

MUELLER: "To avoid the appearance of the fact that death ends what life begins."

CAPTAIN: "Nothing ends and nothing begins. That's the appalling paradox."

MUELLER (sounding pleased): "So you recognize the dilemma?"

CAPTAIN: "The terror beside which death is sweet. To keep from thinking the unthinkable I have studied, worked, read, learned much, accomplished much, all in the approved fashion. I have spared others pain, even to suffering myself. To be busy with good works is the highest good."

MUELLER: "To whistle, hum a tune, pace the floor, count one's heartbeats to ten times ten thousand."

CAPTAIN (weakly): "I have known love."

MUELLER: "Still the paradox intrudes."

CAPTAIN (after a long pause): "Tell me. Who are you?"

MUELLER: "Do you need an answer?"

CAPTAIN: "No."

MUELLER: "Then you know me."

CAPTAIN (wearily): "The voice that whispers from the bottom of the well."

MUELLER: "You have struggled against me, tried to lose me in this dark alley or that crowded street."

CAPTAIN: "One way or another, yet necessarily I believe."

MUELLER: "But no longer. Not now."

CAPTAIN: "Even now."

MUELLER: "There are no roads left. You have travelled them all."

CAPTAIN: "There is one."

MUELLER: "Ah yes, so I must leave you."

CAPTAIN: "The end of our game?"

MUELLER: "The game is ended."

CAPTAIN: "And the loser?"

MUELLER: "I concede. But I made you earn it. Farewell now."

CAPTAIN: "You are still going north?"

MUELLER: "Back to the cold and the darkness, to the land of the unblest barbarians."

CAPTAIN: "Wait. Go with me."

MUELLER: "I have work to do."

CAPTAIN: "Keeping men busy?"

MUELLER: "Spreading the WORD."

CAPTAIN: "The word for no word, the cold beyond panic."

MUELLER: "Only for those I can reach."

CAPTAIN: "Go with me and leave men in peace."

MUELLER: "They will not let me. I am their strength. I will unite them. Eventually."

CAPTAIN (reflecting in the enclosing darkness): "You have been a fearful goader with your fork, a stern disciplinarian."

MUELLER: "Do you regret me?"

CAPTAIN (adrift now in full blackness): "No, not really since . . ."°

MUELLER: "Since what?"

CAPTAIN (fading): ". . . there was . . ."

MUELLER: "Was what?"

CAPTAIN: ". . . no other choice."

EPILOGUE

Hoskins, tears flowing down his grizzled cheeks, stood on the gangway platform staring vacantly at the black Ford panel moving slowly down the dock amid clouds of screaming gulls in startled flight. Near the corner of the warehouse the panel pulled over to let a cab pass through, then disappeared into the alley that led to the street.

Oblivious to the cab and the circling gulls, Hoskins continued to stare after the departed panel. Then suddenly, almost desperately, he jerked a large, checkered blue kerchief from the back pocket of his dungarees, wiped away his tears, then blew his nose angrily. "God damn son-of-a-bitch," he sobbed. "God damn it to hell!"

The cab, a shiny new Checker, pulled up in front of the gangway and a man in a dark blue business suit got out, paid the driver and hurried toward the ship.

"Now who the hell is this?" Hoskins muttered, torn between anger and grief. "Probably the weirdo passenger old Midnight cleaned up the cabin for. Well, he better go right back to where he came from because he won't be goin' nowhere on this old tub."

Before he could yell down to hold the cab, the man, struggling with a big briefcase, a heavy overcoat, and what looked like a portable typewriter, was already puffing up the steep incline. He paused on the deck to get his breath, then introduced himself.

"My name is Mueller, William Mueller." He took an envelope from his pocket and handed it to Hoskins. "Here is my ticket. I'll be going as far as Astoria. However, if the

Caspar is going to call at Portland, I'll stay aboard for the trip up the Columbia River." His low pitched voice was barely audible above the wind. "You must be Captain Larson."

"I'm Hoskins, the chief engineer. If it's the skipper you want, you're just thirty minutes too late."

"But it's only one o'clock," Mueller said. "Mr. O'Hare, the agent, told me you wouldn't be leaving until two or three this afternoon. I had hoped to talk with the Captain before departure and then get to work as soon as possible."

"Talk? Work?"

"I'm from the University Press and we are doing a book on the steam schooners of the West Coast. So far our research is based mainly on Captain Larson's articles in the *Shipping News* and other periodicals. However, since he is the only living authority on the subject we deemed it indispensable to talk with him in the environment he knows so well. From his writings, he appears to be a man of intellect and, at the same time, a warm humanitarian."

"He was all that and more," Hoskins said, gloomily. "He was the only man I ever knew who was afraid of nothing."

"Was?" Mueller asked. "Where is he now?"

"You passed him on your way in. He was in that black Ford panel on his way to the morgue."

The Caspar

Because of the high tide caused by the rains and the heavy south winds, it was possible to tow the old *Caspar* far up into Richardson's Bay before she ran onto the mud. The tug carried her anchor out from the bow and the deckhands shackled her chain onto the mooring bitt. Then they went away and left her to rot.

For many years the *Caspar* lay on the mud. The white paint on her hull and superstructure flaked off and her heavy pine timbers weathered until she looked like an old dead tree trunk.

It was because of the high water when they towed her over that she lay so far away from the other derelicts, although some people around Sausalito say it was because she was so ugly. They had to put her away by herself so as not to spoil the majestic beauty of the big sailing ships like the *Emily F. Whitney* that lay close to town where visitors could admire her tall masts and trim hull. Still others said it was because the *Caspar* didn't have a romantic past like the *Beulah* that ran to Alaska or the City of Papeete that once carried Robert Louis Stevenson to Samoa.

Yet sometimes when I used to row out around the *Caspar* and look at her blunt bow and short masts I wondered if this old steam schooner hadn't had as many adventures hauling lumber up and down the coast as those big square-riggers that sailed so grandly to the Orient or the sleek schooners that carried copra and spices from the Islands.

There was another thing I wondered about. Why did old Hans Grondahl stay aboard the *Caspar* when they left her out in the Bay. The old man was on the boat when they towed her over from San Francisco. He was standing on the foc'sle head and waved to Pederson on the *Sea Ranger* as the tug pulled away.

Old Hans had lived aboard ever since. He used to row over to Sausalito once or twice a week to buy food and tobacco; then he'd go back to the *Caspar*. Sometimes you could see him in his skiff fishing for perch along the rock beach by Belvedere Point. But usually he stayed on the *Caspar*. I had never known anyone to go out to visit him.

Folks around the dock thought he was a little crazy in a harmless way, but no one thought very much about him one way or another. He'd been there so long he was part of the background like the hills around the bay and the weathered old hulls that lay out in the water. I did hear Gustafson say once that he wondered what Old Grondahl would do if the worm-eaten *Caspar* ever broke up in a norther.

During the season of the northers the air is clear and dry. On days like these when the wind is not blowing I like to take my skiff out into the bay and just look around. The hills and Mount Tamalpais which towers above them stand out sharply against the sky, and the water is pure blue. Tall buildings along the skyline of San Francisco and the streets on the hillsides appear to be quite close. The world seems bigger on these days.

It was on such an afternoon that I rowed out to the *Caspar*. I had not been close to the boat for a long time and I could see where planks had fallen off the sides and light shone through the openings. The bow was still high above the water but the stern where the living quarters were had a heavy list. It looked as if she might be broken amidship.

When I came around the after end I saw Old Grondahl. He was in his shirt sleeves leaning on the rail. The faint blue smoke from his pipe drifted out over the water. A lonely figure.

"You've come a long way, son," he said when he saw me in the skiff.

"Yes, but if the wind comes up I'll get back in a hurry."

"It'll blow tonight," he said, "but not till late. Come aboard and have some coffee."

I tied the skiff and climbed up the Jacob's ladder. I noticed that the deck was clean. It looked as if it might just have been holystoned.

Hans Grondahl opened the cabin door and I followed him in. It seemed strange to see the brass door knobs polished. Inside, the cabin was nicely painted. There were oil lamps hanging in gimbals on the bulkheads and several photographs of the *Caspar* taken many years before. In one of them I recognized Grondahl. He had handlebar mustaches and wore an officer's cap. He had a big smile on his face. The picture must have been taken on the after deck just outside the cabin door. Along the forward wall were shelves filled with books. They were mostly big books with large gold titles in raised letters. They looked very old. In one corner of the cabin on an ancient cast-iron wood and coal stove stood a big enameled coffee pot. The coffee smelled good.

Grondahl placed cups on the table and poured the coffee.

"I hope you like it black," he said. "I have no cream."

We sat in silence and drank the coffee. Then to make conversation I remarked:

"It's quite comfortable here. Have you lived aboard the *Caspar* long?"

Old Grondahl did not answer for awhile. Then he said slowly as if mentally adding up the time.

"I was a deck hand on her maiden voyage. I been with her ever since. Fifty-one years."

When I had finished the coffee I stood up and looked out through the porthole. The sun was down behind the mountain and lights had begun to twinkle from the shore. There was a ripple on the water.

"Well, thank you for the coffee," I said. "I should be leaving now. The wind is coming up."

"I'm glad you came," he said. "I believe you are the first."

When I had rowed back to Sausalito I pulled my skiff out of the water and lashed it to the dock. Then I went home and waited for the storm to break.

That night the sky opened up and let the north wind loose. It streaked naked through the valleys of Sonoma and down over the water. It seemed as if not even God could curb the fury of the north wind when it came down over the hills and swept across the bay.

By morning the wind had gone. When I got up I looked out over the bay to see what damage had been done in the night. The big eucalyptus tree at the foot of the hill was down and lay across the power lines. A few fishing boats were up on the beach, and the foremast of the *Emily F. Whitney* lay in the water with a tangle of yards and rigging. The *Caspar* was gone. A dark spot above the water looked as if it might be a bit of her bow.

Down at the dock people stood around looking at the wreckage. Gustafson was there and when I asked him about Old Grondahl he said that most probably he had been drowned. It was just as well, he said, because Grondahl was getting old.

The Albacore Fisherman

The night of the fifth day passed and dawn came dull and gray through the mist that lay over the water. But the coming of the sun brought no change in the appalling blood-warm air. The man, stripped to the waist, could feel neither heat nor cold on his naked skin. The night and the day and the sea and the air were all one deadly sameness.

He stood on the deck close to the wheelhouse watching the albacore lines while the boat pushed on through the oily sea. His eyes followed the long limp curves trailing aft to the little ripples where they dipped into the water. And farther still, past the stern, where he saw the feathered jigs weaving slowly from side to side, yellow and white in the murky greenness. He saw the two divergent waves rolling disconsolately away from the stern, forming an infinite vee that lost itself in the vapid stillness of the sea. From time to time he looked back toward the east where he knew the Island of San Nicolas lay thirty miles across the water. Fifty miles beyond that was Anadapa Island and another twenty-five miles still farther was Santa Barbara on the mainland. But he could see nothing save the thin edged horizon like a ruled line and the pale gray zone of haze above it. In all directions lay the ocean, dull gray and heavy as lead in a mold.

He lifted the cover off the hatch on the after deck and looked down into the fish hold. He could see the rows of albacore, stacked like cordwood, their streamlined bodies, white bellied and black backed, stiff in the melting ice. Their great round eyes glazed, stared obliquely out of the sides of their heads. Down in the bilge the water from the ice splashed between the oak ribs. The ice was melting fast. He knew he would have to head back to Santa Barbara that night.

He put the hatch cover back and stepped over to the bilge pump that was bolted on to the side of the wheelhouse and started pumping out the bilges. The water gushed out of the hose in a clear stream. He pumped with one hand and held the hose with the other letting the water pour over his head and run down his back and over his shoulders. It soaked his pants and ran down into his heavy rubber sea boots but the stinging cold felt good and he flexed the muscles across his chest and breathed deep.

When he finished pumping he went back by the stern and hauled in the port inboard line to clear away the kelp that had caught on the hooks. Long tendrils of slime green sea grass clung to the bulbs on the brown ribbons of kelp. The lukewarm seawater dripped off his wrist onto the deck. He pulled the barbed double hooks out of the tangle of sea grass and kelp, straightened out the feathers and let the line back into the water, being careful that it did not foul the other lines. Then he stood for awhile looking down into the wake. He noticed how the water formed into a hollow like a translucent green cradle close to the transom. The bottom of the hollow was mirror smooth and he could see far down into the torpid gloom below. The propellor pushed up a low mound of water that bubbled and swirled six feet or so aft of the stern. It formed a long straight path of slow turning eddies that faded into the sea toward the east where the land lay.

He went forward again and stood by the wheelhouse. The sun was higher but its light, diffused by the veil of mist, made the sea and the sky one dreary blend of gray and white. His pants, still wet from the icy bilge water, were no longer cold to his flesh. He could feel their damp heaviness clinging to his legs and the thick wool socks soggy and tepid inside his boots.

A hundred yards abeam an albacore leaped. For an instant the full length of its body stood in sharp relief. Close astern he saw another break water. Then one hit on the long dog line that ran to the masthead. The line snapped taut, the shock spring stretched out to full length. He moved across the deck to the stern and pulled on the line with wide-armed strokes, slowly and steadily till the fish was close to the boat. Then with a quick jerk he lifted it up on the deck and hit it a sharp blow between the eyes. The fish stiffened and its mouth opened wide. He twisted the hook out of its mouth and a trickle of dark blood spread out on the deck. Then he picked the fish up by the tail and threw it into the ice hold and went back and dropped the line into the water.

For several hours the boat moved along with the school and the fish came, striking two and three, sometimes five and six lines at once until the man's arms ached and the deck was red with blood and thick with slime from the mouths of fish. Then they were gone and the sea was quiet.

For a while he sat on the hatch and rested. He could hear the barrel-toned exhaust rumbling in the stack on top of the wheelhouse and deep in the hull the velvet drone of the engine. The sun, now well past the zenith, cast a flat lusterless light down through the haze. The sea appeared like a mirror that had been breathed on.

The boat still traveled west, the track of its wake as straight as a plumb line. The man looked back over the water. Sixty, maybe sixty-five miles, he thought, to San Nicolas. Then seventy-five to Santa Barbara. Twelve hours.

He could be in before morning. Next day he would unload, then north to San Simeon, Monterey and the clean cool fog off Frisco.

Suddenly the dog line straightened. He reached for the line and started to pull but the hooks had snagged in a big clump of kelp and the line was tight. As he leaned back against the weight of it the heel of his boot skidded on the slippery deck and his body spun in a half circle. He let go of the line and make a wild leap for the gunn'l. He missed and for an instant he seemed to hang suspended in the air. Then suddenly he felt the warm seawater close over his head.

He flung his arms out trying to catch hold of the dog line but the weight of the sea boots dragged him down. He saw the dark shadow of the kelp slide by, heard the muffled swish of it through the water. He sank deeper. Pale shafts pierced the green gloom around him. He could feel the dull aching pressure of water against his eyes, the wire thin hum in his ears. He tore the knife from its sheath on his belt, slit the boots down to the soles and kicked them off. Then he swam to the surface.

The boat was two hundred yards across the water and moving steadily away. He saw the hull outlined clear and sharp against the gray curtain of sky, the black lettering on the white transom, the empty wheelhouse, the slender bleached outrigger poles like skeleton arms reaching out over the water. Faintly there came the hollow whisper of the exhaust and the low pulsating hum of the engine.

For a moment he half expected the boat to stop or perhaps to circle back. Then slowly, as the boat went on, he felt a dull coldness surge up into his chest and spread out through his limbs. He started swimming, wildly thrashing his arms and kicking his legs. His pants and wool socks dragged in the water. He swam until the humid air burned in his lungs and the blood pounded in his temples. But the boat, gliding smoothly over the water, was getting farther away. He stopped swimming and with great whistling sobs sucked air into his wide open mouth.

The boat was growing smaller now. The black letters on the transom had faded, the bleached outrigger poles were hairlines over the water. In a little while the hollow exhaust and the low hum of the engine merged with the silence and the boat dwindled to a tiny point. All around the sea was quiet and the sun sank lower in the sky.

He could still feel the heavy beat of his heart and a slow throb in his head. He treaded water for awhile and rested. The haze was lifting and vague patches of blue came through. He looked away from the sun toward San Nicolas, around the long level stretch of horizon, searched the water close about him. But he could see nothing save the wide, empty ocean and the darkening sky above.

He thought of the boat heading out to sea with the night coming on. Out there under the stars with the running lights out and the long lines trailing. Moving along steadily in the same straight line. He wondered vaguely why he should think of the running lights and the lines as though he were still aboard.

A strange, uncertain feeling came over him that he was not in the water. That he was not himself. For a moment his mind split and a part of it seemed to stand away. He was on the dock in Santa Barbara telling the story, quietly telling all about it. And the story was real. It had come like a dream comes, out of the darkness, without reason, confused shadows holding no limits. Presently it would go back into the darkness. But the story was real, only the sea and the air were one. They were like nothing and he could feel nothing. Then slowly, like an easy waking he knew that he was there in the water, his hands weaving gently to keep him afloat.

The water had deepened to steel blue and out toward the west the orange-red sun buried itself in the sea. For awhile a spectral line that was umber hued lay low along the ocean's rim and then the darkness hurried westward and spread a shroud across the sky. One by one he saw the stars break through the blackness overhead.

He reached out under the water in a slow breast stroke. Cascades of blue phosphorescence flamed up from his arms. From time to time he saw the fire trails of tiny fish streaking down into the deep or heard the splash of something bigger out in the darkness. Once he heard the even swashing of a shark's tail and saw the white, radium sprinkled water where it churned the surface.

He swam until his arms were tired, then he lay on his back moving his hands slowly. The haze had cleared now and he saw the black depths gleaming with the light of stars that swept across the heavens. The soft, sable blackness of the ocean rose to meet the roundness of the sky. Straight up he could see the seven stars of the Pleiades and north a ways the bowl of the dipper, the handle bent toward Polaris. Lower down in the west where the lesser stars faded he saw the unwinking eye of the planet Venus descending into the sea.

His eyes closed for a moment and when they opened he saw the sky like one great picture—star clouds of the Milky Way, dippers, squares and crosses, the pale twinkle of the Sporades and the infinite black depths of space.

A gentle weariness came over him and his hands moved slower in the half-warmth of the water. He was conscious of the slow, sullen breathing of the sea. The mild night air hung low. He felt it pressing down upon his face.

A water film veiled the brightness of the stars and the whole dome of heaven seemed drifting onward in the void. The night was growing darker with a deeper kind of darkness that reached far out beyond the stars. The night flowed down through time . . . a dark river of night that never ended.

Death of a Hero

Pete was a big fellow, not tall, but wide and thick as a bear, with hands that were big, too, and gnarled and weathered from years at sea. He smoked an old hod of a pipe that seemed built right into his rough, Greek-looking face which was seamed and brown as a block of mahogany. He didn't talk much but when you asked him anything about boats or fishing you could be sure of an answer that was backed up by plenty of experience in all weather and in every kind of boat from little, open double-enders along the Alaska coast to big tuna clippers out of San Diego. Around Sausalito, Pete was considered by the local fishermen not only the best source of reliable information on engine troubles, methods of rigging and handling gear, but a sort of inexhaustible encyclopedia of sea weather, currents and the habits of fish.

Some of the older men like Tom Olsen and Tony Landucci had worked with him on the halibut boats out of Seattle and on the purse seiners and drag boats out of Monterey and around Eureka. And Karl Swenson had been fishing salmon in Alaska the summer of the big storm when Pete had lost his boat and his partner was drowned. They all had stories they liked to tell about his courage, like the time when he jumped into the ocean with a line in his teeth to save a fellow fisherman from the sharks, or when he'd boarded a blazing albacore boat and gotten the crew off and many more, all of which, though Pete rarely talked of these himself, seemed to please him considerably.

To most of the young fellows around the docks who enjoyed boating, or who had boats of their own, or were building boats themselves, or who just hung around the yards because it was good to be there with the smell of pilings and cedar shavings and copper bottom paint, Pete was a kind of hero.

Pete was just the most perfect kind of guy I could have ever met up with, and I hoped sometime to be able to talk him into going outside with me in my boat. Maybe by him being along with me, I thought, I could get over the crazy fear I'd had of the ocean ever since I was a little kid, a real strange feeling I'd probably gotten from all the stories I'd heard about storms and undertows and ships going down and drownings in the surf and all that, but that at the same time had made the ocean seem so fascinating and exciting. I used to dream of getting out there, scared or not, if that makes any sense. Besides, I knew he could teach me more in one trip than I'd be able to learn in a year by myself. Yet, although I had asked him any number of times, he didn't seem interested in going out. Several of the other fellows had asked him, too, but he never would go. "I go out," he'd say, "when I get boat for myself."

And this was apparently what he had in mind. He worked in a brewery up the road and was probably saving his money and looking. He knew every boat on the Bay. But there wasn't one that suited him. Either it was underpowered or overpowered, had too little or too much deck space, or, and this was his most usual comment, "She's not strong." What he was looking for, he said, was a boat "that fits me."

Though he hadn't been out for some time, he always wore black dungarees, a big silver buckle on his belt, a hickory shirt, all nice and clean, and a blue watch cap. His heavy peajacket was usually slung over one big shoulder as he walked about the docks on his days off and talked to the fellows working on their boats. He was sure-footed as a goat and just seemed to float right up a ladder with his jacket hanging on his shoulder and, big as he was, he could jump from one boat to another as light as a feather. Once in a while someone would rib him about the peajacket and watchcap saying, "You look a bit salty there, Pete." But he'd just smile at them good-naturedly behind his short-stemmed pipe. Of course there wasn't a one of us who wouldn't have dressed the same way except we knew we couldn't get away with it.

Every Sunday morning he'd put on his pin-striped suit that always looked too tight on his big muscular body and with his black Fedora hat, a white handkerchief in his lapel pocket, his orange-tan tie, he'd take the ferry over to the city where he went to his Greek Orthodox church to attend the early service.

Since my boat had a fairly roomy cabin with a little pot-bellied stove to keep it warm, quite often of an evening some of the fishermen would row in from their moorings for coffee and some yarn swapping. One night along about the end of summer, Pete and some of the other men dropped by. Tony Landucci had come in earlier with some fish and a couple of crabs and we had cooked up a big cioppino. We'd finished eating and were drinking coffee when Tom Olson asked me when I was going to get started fishing.

"Probably in the spring," I said, "but the fact is, if you want to know the truth of it, I'm kind of scared of that ocean."

"An honest statement if I ever heard one," Tom said, "it's something to be afraid of."

I looked over at Pete who was just sitting there listening but looking like he hadn't heard anything.

"I tell you something," Karl Swenson said, "I been fishing all my life, and I still have plenty respect for the ocean. Some times after bad storm I say to myself, what the hell you want to be fisherman for. I keep going though, like dumb animal. But that storm in the Gulf of Alaska was the worst I ever see. I almost stop fishing then for good."

"You got a good boat," Pete said, "you ride out anything." It was the first time I had ever heard him sound annoyed. "Sure she blow up in the Gulf. But you keep your hand on the tiller, you don't drown. I tell my partner this. But he don't listen. He go below, and put on life jacket and get ready to die. Sure it bad, blow maybe one hundred mile wind. No cloud and full moon. Then we see big rocks. Water break maybe two-three hundred feet up. Oh, sure, she look bad. But there is big hole in rocks with beach in back. My partner get scared then and start to jump. I yell him stay with boat. Goddam storm, I say, but we make it. You watch. But either he don't hear me or he don't believe me. So over he go, and that the last anyone ever see of him. Just about then, big breaker come bustin' in high as mountain and makin' plenty noise too. She pick up that boat like toothpick and away we go. Goddam bastard storm, I say, she bad one. But I don't let loose the tiller, just keep her head up. Then right through the rocks, maybe forty-fifty knots, so fast, I tell you I hardly see nothing except that foam and spray. I nearly bust both arms, but I don't let loose that tiller. Pretty soon she hit sand. Oh, sure, she take out bottom, bust up everything. But I get out alive. Two days I climb rocks, look all over beach. Don't find nothin'. I cry like baby, yell Goddam you devil bastard storm. But I get out alive, I tell you. I do it again too. I get new boat, go back same place, I show not scared of ocean."

Pete was breathing kind of hard when he finished his story. It was pretty clear by then he wasn't really amazed at Karl for his talk of giving up and all but just plain angry at the ocean for wrecking his boat and drowning his partner, the kind of anger you get when your pride has been hurt. So I knew it wouldn't be long now before he'd be back on that same coast proving to himself he could beat his old enemy. And then I got to thinking that it was guys like him that must have been responsible for building up this whole area in the old days, big illiterate guys, but darn smart though, who looked at the mountains and the ocean like they were enemies that had to be beaten down with their bare fists, guys you don't see the likes of much these days because there's not much need for them anymore.

"Why you don't get that big Greek to take you out," Tony said. "He's too dumb to be scared of anythin'."

"Maybe I do just that," Pete said. "Maybe I show this boy you don't know damn thing what you talk about."

Ever since I'd known Pete he'd always seemed a little absentminded, as though he had something else he was thinking about, something more important than whatever it was he was talking about at the time. Now, maybe because he was annoyed, he seemed to be right there. He lit his pipe and really made the smoke go. But pretty soon he was chuckling like something had struck him very funny. Then he began ribbing Karl and Tony about a lot of crazy things that must have happened in the past. And he was laughing like I'd never heard him laugh before.

I didn't really believe he was serious when he said he'd go out with me, but the following Saturday he came down to the boat and began getting things ready. He went through the engine first, changed the points, cleaned the plugs and adjusted the carburetor so the old mill idled down nice and even, and just seemed to purr. Then he went over the steering, tightened up some loose bolts in the quadrant, greased the sheaves and adjusted the tension on the cables. "Steering gear need work," he said, "but she O.K. for good weather. After trip we fix right." When everything seemed in good shape, I got out the salmon gear. The rest of the day and most of Sunday we spent getting all the jigs and weights and lines in order. Then he told me to be ready the following Saturday around about two in the morning, and we'd head up toward Point Reyes and try our luck.

All that week I was as excited as a little kid thinking of how good it would be to quit my job and earn my living fishing. I ran the boat over to the gas dock, and filled the tanks. I washed down the decks and got everything cleared away below. I even cleaned out the bilges and polished what little brass there was in the wheelhouse. It was a great week and full of great feelings. But now and then I'd get to thinking about things that happened when I was a child, like the time when the *Lyman Stewart* went aground in the Gate and my father took me out one gray morning to see how the storm had broken her clean in half with her bow on the beach and her high stern pounding in the waves way out by Mile Rock Light. Then I'd remember the story my mother told me about the wreck of the old *Steamer Bear* on Cape Flattery when she was a young girl and how this woman was thrown up on a rock and nobody could get to her and how she'd sung "Nearer My God to Thee" in the stormy night before she was washed away into the black water. And I'd remember the awful feeling it had given me and how I used to dream about it and wake up at night with the whole dark picture of it in my mind. But right in the middle of it I'd think about Pete and those big hands of his and of how crazy they looked hanging out of the sleeves of his pin-striped suit when he was going to church on Sunday mornings and his big Greek face with that dumb hod of a pipe sticking out of it and right away I'd forget about the other things and feel happy all over again.

Right at two on Saturday morning, Pete was there. I didn't even hear him climb down the ladder and jump over onto the deck. While the engine was warming up, we had some coffee—he was a great one for coffee which he liked boiled down thick and black, like a mug full of road oil. The weather was nice and clear when we pulled out, with some big stars over the hills, and San Francisco just a glow across the Bay. But I could hear the big diaphone blasting from the Bridge, so I figured there must be fog outside. We had the current with us and moved along at a pretty good clip by the docks and ferry slips. There was no wind to speak of until we got past Lime Point. Then a cold breeze came up that was blowing a thin mist through the Gate.

Now I had been all over the Bay, and I'd gone way up into the sloughs. I'd seen some good days and plenty of bad ones too, with heavy winds and rough water. But there was something different about everything once we went under the Bridge. A strange kind of chill was in the air like nothing I'd ever felt in the Bay, a big, dark, cold feeling that seemed to wrap itself right around you. Through the mist, the moon, which was quite low and about at the full, showed dark gray, then bright silver. The black swells that came in from the ocean lifted the boat up like she was nothing at all and went rolling by without a sound. Under the mist, the lights on Mile Rock and Point Bonita to the north were big and bright, and when they swept over the water, the tops of the swells looked wet and shiny as they uncoiled from out of the darkness and went sliding away shoreward. I was standing at the wheel and holding the spokes pretty tight in both hands. Pete was standing beside me. His big hands were in the breast pockets of his pea-jacket. His thick body rolled a little with the movement of the boat, but his booted feet seemed bolted to the deck. In the little light from the binnacle, his dark, Greek face, with its short, black pipe, looked carved out of wood. He was gazing out over the water ahead and seemed quite at home.

Yet, though I'd never been outside before, I knew all about the coast thereabouts, from studying the charts. I knew where channels were and the lights and buoys and all the points and reefs and rocks. So when we cleared Bonita, I kept in the North Channel, far enough out to be safe from the rocks but not so far as to get onto the Four Fathom Bank which is a shallow bar a couple of miles off the point known as the Potatoe Patch. In heavy weather, the seas break and roll over it, and a ship with any draft at all will hit bottom and a small boat would probably have no chance whatever. Of course, in fair weather like we had that morning, there was no danger. But I kept in the channel anyway. By the time the sun came up over the hills along the coast and the light sea mist had cleared, we were well offshore in the area of Point Reyes with our lines down and the engine idling along nicely.

"So you like be fisherman?" Pete asked. We were sitting on the after cabin, watching the lines as the boat rolled pleasantly over the long swells. "You learn things right, you make good money. You never be rich, but you be free. No boss. You in business for yourself. Go north in spring. Go Fort Bragg, Eureka. Go up Alaska if like. In winter, go south. If not like, then stay home. Sleep when wind blow." He was in a fine mood. I'd never seen him look real happy before. Now he just kind of beamed. "Fisherman no have listen to big bull in office," he went on, "eat plenty, make strong man. Sea very pretty too." He pointed with his pipe stem toward the east where the blue water sparkled in the early sunlight. "Sun come up, sun go down. Very pretty. Night time, see plenty stars. Sea smell good too." He took a big breath and let it out slowly. "Sea like good wife. You talk, she listen. Sometimes bad too, like storm in gulf. Wind go crazy, try kill you. Oh, sure, you scared. But who know, maybe that good too."

This was another side of Pete, a side probably few people ever got to see, and I felt kind of proud to be one of them. Just then he reminded me of my eight-year-old brother on one of those times when he wasn't being silly or showing off or raising hell or making stupid faces, but just being serious about something he liked because, at such times, his whole face got beautiful like Pete's was that day, just thoughtful and happy and real peaceful looking.

We trolled all morning and picked up half a dozen silversides and a couple of big king salmon. Around about noon, the wind began to build up, and by four or so was blowing pretty hard. It was about that time we had the first trouble with the engine. Some rust scales from the gas tanks had clogged the screen in the sediment bowl under the carburetor. Pete went below and removed the bowl and cleaned the screen.

"Not good," he said when he came up. "You take out gas, clean tank before go out again." He looked out over the water, then at the shore. "We drift plenty far," he said. "Not good engine stop now."

An old coastal freighter, some distance west of us, was moving in toward the Gate. The smoke from her stack, blowing forward over her bow, made her look like she was going full speed astern. Steep waves were beginning to run over the big swells. Here and there the tops broke, making nasty little flecks of white on the blue-black water.

"Go in now," Pete said. "Pretty soon blow very hard."

I spun the wheel around and headed back toward the Gate. Pete went aft, brought in the lines and secured things on deck. The old freighter had altered her course, and was cutting across our bow maybe half a mile ahead. I could see her rusty iron plates daubed with red lead and the big white spray from forward as she plunged into the rising seas. The sky was quite clear, and the sun, which had been slanting downward, suddenly got big and red. And then, almost as I watched, it eased itself right down into the limpy water along the horizon. The old freighter's mast head light came on and high above, the full moon shone kind of cold and white in the clear evening sky. The swells were so big by now, that when the boat was in the troughs, everything disappeared completely. I changed my course a few degrees figuring to follow the freighter, which was heading for the north channel, close in to Point Bonita.

"We stay outside Potatoe Patch," Pete said. He had come into the wheelhouse and was standing beside me at the wheel. "North Channel no good now. If engine stop, we go on rocks." He filled his pipe and lighted it. His big, tanned face was as calm as if he were sitting on the dock on a quiet Sunday afternoon talking about net-mending or the benefits of a fisherman's union. And feeling his calm and confidence, somehow I wasn't afraid either. He was a great guy and a great teacher too, I thought, as I changed the course again, this time heading out well to the west of the Potatoe Patch which I could see now in the moonlight, some four or five miles ahead, was beginning to churn up white.

Everything went well for the next half hour or so despite the wind which was howling down from astern at almost gale force. I managed to ease her out in the big quartering seas so we could clear the bar by a good mile or more. Now and then a wave would break and wash over the after deck which, if I'd been alone would have scared the hell out of me. But with Pete there, the whole thing was kind of exciting. My fear was gone. Even my muscles seemed to get stronger. I stood with my legs apart and spun the wheel about, keeping the boat from getting broadside in the troughs. I revv'd up the engine and drove the hull forward over the black hills that raced down on us from out on the ocean like I'd been doing it all my life. It was a great feeling, the best and biggest feeling I'd ever known.

I don't know how far we were from the Potatoe Patch, maybe a mile, maybe less, when the engine stopped the second time. It coughed once, picked up again, sputtered, then died completely. In an instant, Pete was out of the wheelhouse and down below. The boat with no headway now, went wild, bobbing and tossing, lifting, and falling. The wind had a heavy sound like a big wave rushing up on a beach. The water itself didn't make much noise, just a hissing sound with now and then a kind of snapping. Pete hollered up for a flashlight. With the boat flying around the way it was, it took much longer to clean out the screen and get the bowl back on than before. I crawled up into the wheelhouse again with Pete close behind me and started the engine. Then I looked ahead. Not a hundred yards away, a huge wave broke and crashed. Beyond, in the bright moonlight, as far as I could see, was nothing but seething white water.

"Pete," I yelled.

But he was not there. The door to the wheelhouse swung open then banged shut. Suddenly I remembered the steering quadrant. Good Christ, he'd gone out on deck! I pulled back on the throttle and started to bring the boat about. But it was too late. Another wave picked her up and just threw her right into the boiling foam of the Potatoe Patch.

For the next few minutes, or hours, or years—I can't remember what happened to time—I just hung on to the wheel. The moon was scribbling white lines all over the black sky. I could hear the crash and boom of breakers all around and the engine labor as the boat climbed the steep slope of some gigantic wave, then race at full throttle, as she dived, almost vertically downward, into a deep through.

Suddenly the boat spun broadside to the seas and began to drop like it was going right to the bottom. Down, down, down. Then something exploded overhead; the cabin door was ripped from its hinges; black water rushed in through the broken wheelhouse windows. I was still hanging on to the wheel, but the violent shock of that massive wave crushing down from above threw me against the after bulkhead with such force that for a minute I must have been knocked unconscious. When I managed to get back to the wheel, the boat was out of the Potatoe Patch. The big wave that had smashed down on her must have picked her up again and thrown her off the bar just like the one before had thrown her on. I looked out on deck for Pete. In the moonlight, the deck was empty. I shouted his name. There was no answer. I shouted again. My throat seemed like it had a rope around it. I crawled out through the doorway, screaming into the wind. Still there was no answer. Then I realized he had been washed over. Oh Christ! I jumped to the wheel and was about to turn back. But I knew right away that that would be useless. The chance of finding him on that wild bar was next to impossible. Suddenly all my strength seemed to go. I leaned against the wheel aching all over and kind of empty inside.

Though the bar had broken the force of the waves, the swells were monstrous and the wind howled louder than ever. Dead ahead the big light on Bonita flashed twice over the stormy water, then eclipsed. Beyond, I could see the long chain of yellow lights on the Bridge and beyond that, the soft glow of the city inside the Gate. I set a course directly under the center of the Bridge and began slowly to unbutton my shirt, which was soaked.

Suddenly my insides began to twist up in a knot. God Almighty! Pete was back there somewhere in the middle of that white whirlpool! Oh, Jesus! Goddam bastard Potatoe Patch! I shook the wheel with all my strength and pounded my foot on the deck. I could feel the hot tears on my face. Goddam bastard, I kept shouting. Then a thought came to me. Maybe with all his strength, he could have kept alive. Maybe he'd gotten through it and was, right at that moment, floundering around in the waves on this side. I started to turn the boat around but realized again how hopeless it would be. Then I remembered the flares in the locker below. I'd pull into the cove behind Bonita and signal the Coast Guard. There might be a chance, one in a million, but maybe, with their big lights and all, they might be able to find him. I swung the wheel over and with the waves bearing down broadside, rolling the boat over so the gunnel and half the cabin was awash, I headed, with the throttle wide open, for the cove in the lea of Bonita.

In a matter of minutes, I was in the lea of the point. I threw the engine out of gear and cut the throttle. Suddenly it was very quiet, only the crashing of waves and the high sound of the wind. I had just started down the companion-way to the cabin when I heard a strange sound from below. I stopped to listen. It was a low mumbling, like a voice from underwater. And it came from the cabin! I dropped down quietly and switched on the light.

And there was Pete! He was down on his knees by the bunk. A life jacket was strapped onto his back; another was clutched in his arms. He did not look up but went right on praying in a kind of low sing-song, with his head bent down. His watch cap was gone, and his hair, which I had never seen before, was gray with a bald patch in the middle. I switched off the light, went back to the wheelhouse and headed the boat in toward the Bridge once more.

Once inside, the storm stopped as if by magic. The Bay off Sausalito was flat calm. I tied up at the dock and turned off the engine. The moon had gone down behind the hills, but by the night lights on the dock, I could see the ripped out door and the shattered wheelhouse windows. I stood back in the shadow inside. In a little while, Pete came up. He had taken off his life jacket. He did not look at me, but stepped out on deck without making a sound. I watched him pull the boat in and jump over onto the ladder. One foot missed the lower rung, and his leg went into the water. Then he climbed slowly and kind of heavily up onto the dock. I went out on deck and watched him walking slowly between the stacked lumber and winches and shored-up boats. His head was bent down and his arms hung kind of straight by his sides. He stopped for a moment by a big halibut boat under a cargo light by the boat shop. I could see him quite clearly. He looked up at the high bow, then reached up and ran his hand over the smooth lines of the forward part of the hull. A moment later, he disappeared in back of the old storage shed. I stayed there awhile longer, then went below. I turned in quickly, but exhausted as I was, I could not sleep.

The next day, and for a good while after, the boat was a kind of showpiece, with the windows all broken, the running lights torn off and wires hanging from the splintered end of the mast. Of course, I had to tell everyone the whole story a hundred times and answer all their questions.

When they asked me about Pete, I said he was right with me all the way through and that I'd have never made it without him, which was the truth.

I never saw Pete again. Karl Swenson said he'd seen him getting on the ferry early the following morning. He was dressed up in his Sunday clothes and was carrying a suitcase. Karl had hollered at him, but he hadn't answered. As far as I know, he has never been seen around Sausalito since.

AFTERWORD
by Jerome Gold

LES GALLOWAY and
THE FORTY FATHOM BANK

In 1980, out of money, I took a break from graduate school and went back into the army. I thought I would be stationed in Hawaii but found myself at Fort Baker, on the Sausalito side of San Francisco Bay, and living in the Bachelor Officers Quarters at Presidio. Evenings, I would take a book and walk out to one of the restaurants off post for a cup of coffee. It was important to get away from the army at least once a day if I could.

The first time I saw Les Galloway was in the International House of Pancakes, the IHOP, on Lombard. I was sipping coffee over a book and I heard two people talking about writing. One, a twentyish, black-haired waitress, was saying how much she loved to write, that she wrote every day in her journal and she wrote poetry too. Her writing meant everything to her, she said. She was telling this to an older man dressed in a windbreaker and work pants and seated in a booth at an angle to mine. A manuscript was spread out on the table in front of him.

The man said he did not write poetry. He wrote fiction, although he had written a teleplay on Mark Twain once that had been produced. He started talking craft and authors to her, but she only said again how much her own writing meant to her. Continuing to eavesdrop, I understood that the man knew what he was talking about and seemed to have a lot more experience than I had. When the waitress left I thought about going over and introducing myself to him, but I was unable to think of something to say beyond the introduction and so I let the moment pass.

A couple of weeks later I saw him again, this time in the cafeteria at Presidio. In those days the army ran the cafeteria, but the Presidio was an open post and the cafeteria was open to civilians. Les was a small man with thin white hair and a right leg shorter than his left. He used a cane as he walked into the building and he carried a brown paper shopping bag in his other hand. He set the bag down at a vacant table and then got himself a cup of tea and an English muffin and returned to his table with his tray. From his bag he extracted a papaya and a lime. He glanced around the room but did not see me watching him. At least his eyes did not stop at mine. He cut the papaya into halves with a serrated butter knife and then he cut the lime into halves. He scraped the seeds out of the papaya and placed them on a paper napkin on his tray and folded the napkin over them. Then he squeezed lime juice onto the yellow fruit. I would later learn that this was habitually his lunch. Tea or maybe coffee and maybe a muffin, but always a papaya with lime or occasionally a scoop of vanilla ice cream, which he would buy at whatever restaurant he was in. He always carried the papaya and the lime in the bag with him, regardless of what restaurant he went into, and in the bag also were manuscripts he was working on and a few books, though all I ever saw him read in a restaurant, other than a manuscript, was the newspaper.

When he was almost finished with the papaya I walked over to his table and introduced myself. I told him I'd seen him talking with the waitress at the IHOP but he didn't remember her or what he had said to her. Still, he was friendly and when I asked if I might sit down with him, he agreed readily.

I told him that I also wrote. When I said this his eyes lost their quizzicality and fixed themselves on me. He mentioned some things about craft and technique and I commented on what he said, and he thought about what I had said and commented back. And so we began to trust each other.

He said he had written a novel that he had not been able to place with a publisher. It was titled *The Forty Fathom Bank*. It was too short for a book, editors said, and too long for a story. One journal in the Pacific Northwest had accepted it, then bumped it for a story by Joyce Carol Oates. The editor said if Les could reduce it from one hundred pages to six the magazine would publish it. Les refused and decided that he could not stand Joyce Carol Oates' writing.

He did not like Henry Miller either, did not like him personally. Once, in the fifties, Les was in a jazz bar when Henry Miller and his wife came in. There were a couple of empty chairs at Les's table and Miller asked if they could sit there. After the set, they talked about this and that and then about writing and Les said something witty, catching Miller by surprise. Miller turned to his wife and said, "Isn't it amazing what you can find in some of these places?" Les never forgave him that, that arrogance that placed him at a station below Miller's own, and he had not read any of Miller's work since.

He did like Dreiser's work and he liked Djuna Barnes' *Nightwood* and said she had really known Paris whereas Hemingway had not, though how he could know who had known what, he did not say. He liked Jean Rhys' writing. I had not read her and he said he would lend me a couple of her books. We agreed to meet the next Saturday and exchange manuscripts.

We met again at the Presidio cafeteria. I handed over a manuscript copy of my novel, *The Negligence of Death*, and he gave me a copy of *The Forty Fathom Bank* and a book by

Jean Rhys, *Good Morning, Midnight*. He settled in to eating his papaya while I read the first paragraphs of his manuscript. I could see it was something I would want to pay attention to and I set it aside, telling Les I would read it later in my room. He had been watching me as he ate and after I said this he relaxed and said he would read my book later too, when he was alone.

We talked writing again. He had had a story published in *Esquire* back in the forties, and another one in *Prairie Schooner*. He was not enthusiastic about academic publications because nobody read them, he said, but he was pleased that *Prairie Schooner* had done "Where No Flowers Bloom." We sat for a while without speaking. He puffed at the pipe he was trying to light.

It was an exceptionally clear day, I remember, and as we looked out at the bay through the big windows Les remarked how close the land on the other side appeared when the sun was out and there was no mist. He used to teach fiction writing at Fort Mason, he said, and he once had a student, an elderly woman, who had been a little girl at the time of the San Francisco earthquake and fire. Her mother had taken her out on a ferry with other people fleeing the fire and the ferry had brought them all out to the middle of the bay where it was safe and had stopped so they could see the city burn. She told the class seventy years later how it had looked, the city burning down to the water, how she had seen the section where her house had been all red with the fire's glow, how worried she had been about her father and her brother who had stayed behind. She had held the class in thrall when she told this, but she did not write a word about it. Instead, she wrote light romances.

Les and I got together again the following week. Each of us had wonderful things to say about the other's work. His little book seemed to me a near-perfect piece of writing. The character development was solid, and the book had a theme! I was not accustomed to recent American novels, other than some science fiction, having something to say about the nature of our species. I told Les this. He came back with "Character and theme are everything. If you have character and theme, everything else will follow." He wagged his finger at me as though he were a schoolmaster trying to impress his student to remember something.

I asked Les about Conrad. It seemed to me that *The Forty Fathom Bank* was a kind of converse of *The Secret Sharer.* Les said he had read *Heart of Darkness* while writing his book and thought that might have been an influence. I mentioned *The Secret Sharer* again but Les only shrugged.

In 1982 I left the army and returned to Seattle to finish graduate school. In the fall I went to Samoa to do anthropological fieldwork. While there I met an American who, though earning his living as a teacher in Samoa, was also an editor for a small press in Milwaukee. It had published one book and on its title page was "Milwaukee and Pago Pago," which meant that while John lived in (or near) Pago Pago, the other editor lived in Milwaukee. The book they had published had been written by the Milwaukee editor. John said they were looking for other manuscripts. I wrote to Les, asking him to send me *The Forty Fathom Bank.* I gave it to John as soon as I received it. He liked it very much and sent it to his co-editor. They had an arrangement whereby both had to agree to publish a book; neither had the authority to acquire a book on his own.

The Milwaukee editor turned it down. The rejection letter was perfunctory, but he told John that if Les were a younger man he would be willing to publish the book, but Les was not young.

John was dumbfounded and I was angry. To both of us a book was to be judged by its quality. The press finally died because John's friend would not agree to publishing a second book.

From this experience and listening to John I had learned some of the rudiments of publishing. He had been an editor for the University of California at Berkeley and was a poet and literary critic, so he knew publishing, at least certain aspects of it, from both the publisher's vantage point and the author's.

When I returned to the United States I went to San Francisco to see Les. I suggested we publish his book ourselves. Les equivocated. He did not like the idea of being both author and publisher. My argument was this: Editors select books for publication that fall within the parameters set by the companies they work for. Les and I both knew he had written a good book. Quality was not the issue. The issue was the acquisition policies of the large publishing houses. Still, Les was unsure. Finally I said: "How will you feel five years from now if you don't do it?" And so we put together our own press, Black Heron Press, to publish *The Forty Fathom Bank.* The book appeared in 1985.

As a boy, Les had developed a high fever and had to be hospitalized. He never learned the nature of the fever but it left him with a stiffened hip and a leg that would not grow much longer. Ater high school he sailed to the South Pacific on the last clipper ship put out of San Francisco. Later, he dropped out of the University of California to go to South America. He was a motorcycle courier for a Bolivian general during a war against Paraguay, but always an admirer of competence, he deserted because he did not think the general knew what he was doing. Following travels in South America, Les lived in Mexico City for a year. Except for on unpublished novel, *Beyond the Dark Mountain,* much of which concerns a Pacific voyage, he did not write about any of this. Instead, he wrote some exquisite stories about the sea, including *The Forty Fathom Bank,* "Where No Flowers Bloom," and "The Albacore Fisherman."

He began work on *Beyond the Dark Mountain* when he was sixty finishing it almost ten years later. He met with the usual responses when he sent it out: editors did not read it but pretended they had and sent it back, or they did not send it back. Mostly they ignored it. Finally an editor from a local publishing house did read it and liked it and offered Les a contract. The week before they were to begin editing, the entire fiction staff, including Les's editor, was fired. The publisher had decided to cease publishing fiction. Three or four years later, Les told me that he had been disappointed and angry, but he had also felt relieved. Publishing that book, he believed, would have changed his life and he did not want it to change. He continued sending the manuscript around but nothing happened and I think he regarded sending it out as a matter of duty rather than desire. We never talked about publishing it through Black Heron Press, if for no other reason than that it was very long and we could not have afforded it. The novel remains unpublished.

Until he became too ill to write, he worked on another novel, a kind of love story. (One must always qualify the genre with Les: *The Forty Fathom Bank* is a kind of sea story but also it is a tale of greed and the failure of redemption.) I never saw it, and as far as I know, no copy exists. Convinced by a friend that the story was not up to the standard Les set with *The Forty Fathom Bank* and the best of his stories, he destroyed it.

⁘⁘⁘⁘⁘⁘⁘⁘⁘

I knew Les for only the last ten years of his life. He wrote well until a year or two before he died, when physical pain and medication confounded that special clarity of mind he needed to write. His last decade, it seems to me, was an itemized giving-up of everything that was important to him, including any attempt to resolve the conflicts that had beset him early on. His writing showed no resolution. (Were he able to read these last sentences, his eyes would flash and he would turn away in contempt. "Writing is not about resolution," he would say. "It is about conflict, and conflict is never resolved.") His late writing showed, instead, wonderment and knowledge. He believed in Nothing as though it were Something. Yet despair was foreign to him. Writing for a few friends, he told me, was enough. Had anyone else said this, I would not have believed him. But Les was so lacking in self-mercy that I took him at his word. He did that, writing for his friends, as long as he was able.

One night the phone rang at half past midnight and I thought immediately of Les. Who else would call at that hour? I did not want to get out of bed, and I let the machine take the call. I listened for a voice and when it didn't come, I was even more certain that it was he, for he hated talking to my machine. I promised myself that I would call him back but I didn't. When I had talked with him a week or two earlier, he had sounded so depressed—he was weak from the dialysis, he said—that I was reluctant to talk with him again so soon. He had asked when I would be coming down from Seattle to San Francisco. I told him I did not think it would be before August or September and he said he did not think he would be alive then. I had never heard him sound so tired. I did not try to joke with him. We talked a little about books and then we hung up.

On Thursday, May 3, 1990, a message from his daughter Lisa was on my machine when I came home from work. Les had died the Sunday before. It was a stroke. He had expected to die from an aortic aneurysm he had been cultivating.

Instead, it was a blood clot that had traveled to his brain from his foot.

⁘⁙⁘⁙⁘⁙⁘⁙⁘

A final vignette, told to me by a friend of Les. In the late eighties when *The Forty Fathom Bank* had been out for several years, he and Les had gone to dinner at a very good fish place in San Anselmo, California. It was a weekend evening and the restaurant was packed, the tables pushed so closely together that you could not help but hear your neighbors' conversation. At the table nearest Les was a couple engrossed in talk about fishing and books. They were young, in their earliest twenties, but they knew what they were talking about. Les figured the young man must be a commercial fisherman, and both he and his woman friend knew the best books about the sea. Before either of them could object, Les had joined in their conversation, and in a moment the young man turned to him and said, "Oh, next you'll be telling us you're the author of *The Forty Fathom Bank*!"

I can visualize Les's reaction: his eyes take on a sudden shine, his mouth falls open just a little, in surprise and delight, but in wonder, too, at how the world works. And he says, the lines in his face smoothing into a smile, "Why, yes, I am."

Having recently reread *The Forty Fathom Bank,* I was impressed again by its classic structure. Each character acts out of personal longing, his desire converging with the desire of the opposing character, both blind to what must happen, so as to create a tragedy. Though the story is told in first person, the reader has the sense that the author is not telling a tale but relating the events leading up to a disaster. Tragedy and individual want were Les's forte. If he had written nothing else, the perfect lines of this small book would be enough to ensure its place in the literature of the English language.